Abby was shocked at her own response

She could think of nothing as Piers's lips crushed her own.

"Let me go, Piers," she panted. "We're equal now. I've proved my point, and you've proved you still have feelings."

"Feelings!" Piers's hand forced her face up. "What do you know about my feelings? You almost crippled them eleven years ago."

"That—that's what you believe," she choked, trying to prize his fingers from her face. "Piers, let me go. I didn't intend this to go so far."

"*You* didn't intend," he mocked harshly. "What did you intend?" He paused. "Are you curious to find out how good we still are together?"

"No!" Abby was appalled, but Piers was serious.

"Why not? It's what we both want."

ANNE MATHER
is also the author of these

Harlequin Presents

and these

Harlequin Romances

Many of these titles are available at your local bookseller.

For a free catalog listing all titles currently available,
send your name and address to:

HARLEQUIN READER SERVICE
1440 South Priest Drive, Tempe, AZ 85281
Canadian address: Stratford, Ontario N5A 6W2

ANNE MATHER

season of mists

Harlequin Books

TORONTO • NEW YORK • LOS ANGELES • LONDON
AMSTERDAM • PARIS • SYDNEY • HAMBURG
STOCKHOLM • ATHENS • TOKYO • MILAN

Harlequin Presents first edition November 1982
ISBN 0-373-10546-0

Original hardcover edition published in 1982
by Mills & Boon Limited

CHAPTER ONE

THE letters were waiting for her when they got back to the flat.

It had been an awful day. First the blow that Bourne Electronics was about to close, then the call from Matthew's form-master, asking her to come and see him after school, and now these two letters, postmarked Rothside, and bringing back memories Abby would have rather forgot.

Matthew followed her into the tiny living room of the flat, flicking a glance at the letters in her hand before flinging himself carelessly on to the chintz-covered sofa. He was a tall boy for his age, easily five feet six inches, and already on eye-level terms with his mother, which did not make for easy admonishment. But right now, Abby was more concerned about the reason why Piers should be writing to her after so long than with the latest chapter in her son's chequered school career. Matthew was a problem child, or at least within the past two years he had become so, and she was rapidly losing faith in her own ability to control him.

It didn't used to be like that. For ten years they had been close, very close. And then he had discovered that his father was still alive, that contrary to the stories his mother had told him since he was a baby, his father was not dead, and everything had gone wrong from that time on.

Abby had tried to exonerate herself. She had tried to explain that her reasons for keeping his parentage a secret was to save him from the very feelings of rejection he was suffering now, but Matthew had refused to listen. When he learned that she had, in fact, left his father before he was born, he refused to listen to any explanations, blaming her entirely for the breakdown of her marriage.

To begin with, Abby had not forced the issue. She had believed that given time, Matthew would come round, would try to understand, would forgive her. But it hadn't worked that way. Time had not healed, it had festered, and the deterioration in their relationship—and in Matthew's school behaviour—could be measured from that date.

But now, the news that unless her son stopped playing truant and started attending lessons with the intention of learning something, she would be asked to remove him from the school, took second place to the need to know why her husband should have written to her. Piers never wrote. From time to time, she had word of him via Aunt Hannah. But since his visit to the hospital after Matthew was born, he had never contacted her direct, and in spite of all the years between, Abby's fingers shook as she slit the envelope open.

It was strange, she thought, how she could remember his handwriting after so long. But then perhaps not so strange when she considered the long hours she had spent translating his scrawled script into neatly-typed letters and reports. She had enjoyed typing for him, she remembered unwillingly. She had enjoyed the thrill of going to the Manor every morning, and working in the elegant luxury of the library. All the other girls had envied her, working for Piers Roth, who was something of a heart-throb around Rothside and Alnbury. She had basked in the glory of landing such a marvellous job, and when Piers had started to show his attraction to her, she had seen her life developing like some wonderful romantic novel, where she and Piers fell in love, and married, and lived happily ever after . . .

The letter emerged from its envelope, the paper thick and vellum-bound, bearing the familiar address in the centre of the page at the top.

Dear Abby . . .

'Who's it from?' Matthew, sprawled on the couch, his closely-cropped fair hair reminding her of pictures she had seen of the inmates of a prison camp, was regarding her with unusual curiosity. Perhaps he had noticed the way her hand was shaking, she thought, moving to the window as if she needed more light. It was something for him to address her without being spoken to first.

'Give me a moment,' she said, not yet prepared to make the ultimate sacrifice of telling him, and Matthew shrugged and studied the white laces in his black boots.

Dear Abby, she read again, drawing a deep breath, *You will probably not be entirely surprised to learn that I have decided to divorce you.*

Divorce! Abby found she was not just surprised, she was stunned. Somehow, foolishly she now realised, she had begun to believe Piers was never going to seek a divorce. Perhaps, in the back of her mind, she had even nurtured the hope that one day this whole awful mess would be resolved and Piers would believe her story. But now, it seemed that she was wrong, and the words he had used stung her unpleasantly.

She read on:

I realise I had no need to inform you of my intentions in the circumstances, but I wanted you to know that I no longer feel any hostility towards you. What's done is done. You were too young to be tied down to matrimony, and I was old enough to know better.

Abby's teeth were digging into her lower lip now, but she forced herself to finish reading.

I trust you and the boy are both well. You will be hearing from my solicitors within the next few days. Yours, etc. Roth.

Just Roth, thought Abby bitterly, folding the page. Not Piers, or even Piers Roth; just Roth: as if he was writing to some business acquaintance. Her jaw quivered, but just for a moment. Then she steeled her emotions. So what? she asked herself severely. What difference would it make to her? She would still call herself *Mrs* Roth. Nothing could alter that. So why did she feel so abysmally shattered?

'Well?'

She had forgotten Matthew for a moment, but now she glanced at him over her shoulder. 'It's nothing,' she said, pushing the letter back in its envelope. 'Nothing important, that is. Oh—and this one's from Aunt Hannah.'

'If she's my aunt, how come I never meet her?' Matthew countered, swinging his feet to the floor. Then he pulled a face. 'Oh, don't tell me, I know. She lives in Northumberland, and we can't afford to go all that way to see her.' He grimaced. 'What you really mean is, that's where my father lives, too, and that's why we never visit her. Because you're afraid I'll meet him!'

'No!'

Abby's cheeks flushed, but she knew he didn't believe her. Matthew would never believe the truth, even if she told it to him. He was firmly convinced she had deprived him of his father by running away to London.

Turning back to Aunt Hannah's letter, Abby scanned the unsteady print with smarting eyes. The letter was shorter than usual. Just one page, instead of the half dozen or so Aunt Hannah usually wrote. Her letters tended to be epistles, describing every small incident that happened in Rothside, with an attention to detail born of loneliness; and although Abby told herself she only read the letters to please the old lady, secretly she devoured every word.

Hannah Caldwell was not in fact her aunt, but her mother's, but when Abby's mother had died giving birth to a stillborn child, she had brought the little girl to Rothside to stay with her. Abby's father had been terribly distraught over his wife's death, and after selling their house in Newcastle, had moved to Scotland, to work in Aberdeen. It had been arranged between him and Aunt Hannah that Abby should join him when he had found a house and obtained a housekeeper. But it never came off. Laurence Charlton was drowned in a sailing accident only a few weeks later, and Abby's visit with Aunt Hannah became permanent.

Now she viewed the old lady's letter with growing concern. It appeared that Aunt Hannah had had a heart attack only ten days ago. *Nothing serious, you understand,* she wrote, with endearing understatement, *just a reminder that I'm not as young as I used to be.*

Abby shook her head. How old was Aunt Hannah now? Eighty-two, eighty-three? She frowned. Too old to be living alone in the cottage, she thought anxiously, particularly if her heart was not strong.

Doctor Willis is talking of moving me into Rosemount, the letter continued, *but I told him he'd have to carry me out of here on a stretcher. That's all these young doctors can think about these days—herding old people into homes, so that they can be lumped together like cattle. I don't want to live with a lot of old fogies. I like young people around me. I just wish you and Matthew lived a little nearer. I do miss you, Abby.*

Abby's conscience smote her. It had been hard on Aunt Hannah, she knew that. Her marriage to Piers, when she was only eighteen, had been hard enough for the old lady to bear, but at least she had believed Abby would be happy. Then, Abby's leaving Rothside less than a year later had changed all that, and Aunt Hannah had blamed herself for allowing it to happen. Of course, in the beginning, when Matthew was just a baby, she had made an occasional trip to London to see her great-great-nephew, but inevitably the cost—and her advancing age—had made the journey impossible. It was almost ten years since they had met, and although Abby corresponded regularly, she knew it was not the same.

And now this—Aunt Hannah having a heart attack, and Abby not learning about it until the old lady was able to write and tell her. She was her only relative, after all. And she owed her a lot for the way she had looked after her all those years ago.

Sighing, she turned to the last few lines of the letter:

You'll have heard, no doubt, that Piers is planning on marrying again.

Abby blinked. The divorce!

He called to see me a few days ago, her aunt went on. *I expect Doctor Willis had told him about my little bit of trouble, and he walked in, large as life, with a basket of fruit and some lovely brown eggs from the home farm. I said he shouldn't have bothered, but he insisted it was no trouble, and I suspect he wanted to warn me, before I heard the news officially. It's Valerie Langton, of course. You remember, I told you the Langtons bought Manor Farm, after Ben Armstrong retired. She's a pretty thing, not much more than twenty-three or four, and she should suit Mrs Roth, seeing that she's fond of hunting and charity work.*

Well, my dear, I haven't the strength to write any more now. Do write soon. You know how much I look forward to your letters. All my love . . .

Abby found she was breathing rather heavily as she replaced her aunt's letter in its envelope. So Piers wanted a divorce so that he could get married again. She couldn't help the sudden surge of resentment that gripped her. How could he? she asked herself, how could he?

Aware that Matthew was still watching her, she forced herself to behave normally. 'Aunt Hannah's had a heart attack,' she declared, taking off the jacket of the suit she had worn to work. 'The doctor thinks she shouldn't be living alone at her age, and I'm inclined to agree with him.'

Matthew shrugged. 'So why doesn't she come and live with us?' he asked practically.

Abby sighed. 'Because she wouldn't want to leave her home. And besides,' she took a deep breath, 'I couldn't afford to offer her a home. Bourne Electronics is closing down. I'm going to be out of a job in less than a month.'

Matthew's eyes widened. 'So what will you do?'

'I don't know.' Abby hadn't had time to think of her own troubles yet. What with being summoned to Matthew's school, and Piers' letter, not to mention Aunt Hannah's heart attack, she had been diverted from what was arguably the most serious problem of all.

What was she going to do? This flat was small, but the rent was exorbitant, and any reduction in their weekly income was bound to create difficulties. They lived a hand-to-mouth existence as it was, each week's pay spoken for, almost as soon as it was handed over. What with gas and fuel bills, Matthew's clothes, which were a continual drain on her resources, and the need to keep herself as smart as the secretary to the managing director should be, food came way down on their list; and in spite of the cost, she was glad to pay for Matthew's school dinners, which at least ensured that one of them had a decent meal every day. Abby herself ate little. She was lucky enough not to need a lot of food, and her tall slim figure had scarcely altered since her schooldays. Indeed, Trevor said she did not look old enough to have a son of Matthew's age, but Abby took his compliments with a generous measure of salt. Trevor was biased, and no matter what he said, Abby was convinced she had aged considerably over the past two years.

But now she faced her son with real anxiety. What would they do? What *could* they do? And how would Matthew react if there wasn't even enough money to allow him his weekly pocket money?

'Will you get another job?'

Matthew was evidently concerned, and Abby strove to reassure him. 'I hope so,' she said, trying to speak lightly. 'I'll have to, won't I, as I'm the breadwinner.'

Matthew scuffed his boot against the rug. 'I wish I was old enough to get a job,' he muttered. 'Another four years! It's not fair!'

Abby did not answer him, but walked determinedly into the tiny kitchen that opened off the living room. She had yet to face the prospect of Matthew leaving school at sixteen. Once, she had had confidence in his doing well in his exams and earning a place at a university. Now, she held out no such hopes, even if she had been able to save the money to afford it. Matthew was simply not interested in learning anything. The gang he ran around with only just avoided contact with the law, and she dreaded to think what would happen when he left school. She didn't want a tearaway for a son. She wanted a simple, ordinary boy; one who respected her as she respected him, and did not spend his days blaming her for ruining his chance in life.

She was filing some letters a few days later, when the phone started to ring in her office. Leaving the filing room, she hurried back to her desk to pick up the phone, and knew a moment's foreboding when the telephonist said the call was for her. Not Matthew's form-master again, she prayed silently, closing her eyes, and then opened them again when a strange masculine voice said: 'Mrs Roth? Sean Willis here, Mrs Roth—Miss Caldwell's doctor.'

Abby's mouth went dry. 'She's not——'

'No, no, nothing to worry about, Mrs Roth. At least, not immediately, that is.'

'Not immediately?' Abby was confused.

'I'm explaining myself badly, Mrs Roth. Actually, why I'm ringing is because Miss Caldwell tells me you're her only relative. Is that right?'

'Her only relative.' Abby was endeavouring to regain her composure. For one awful moment she thought Dr Willis had been about to tell her that Aunt Hannah was dead, and that would have been the last straw. 'I—yes. Yes, I believe I am,' she agreed now. 'Why? Is something wrong? What can I do?'

'I'm hoping you'll be able to persuade her to leave Ivy Cottage,' replied Dr Willis heavily. 'She lives alone, as you know, and just recently she suffered a mild heart attack.'

'I know. She wrote and told me.'

'Good. Then you'll realise how foolish it is of her to insist on staying at the cottage. Good heavens, she's over eighty! Anything could happen.'

'What are you saying, Dr Willis? That Aunt Hannah is ill? That she should be in hospital?'

'In hospital, no. Rosemount, yes. I don't know whether you know this, but Rosemount is a rather pleasant residential home——'

'—for old people,' Abby finished dryly. 'Yes, she told

me that, too. But I'm afraid she doesn't want to leave her home.'

Dr Willis sighed. 'If you care about your aunt, Mrs Roth, you'll understand how important it is for her to have constant supervision. If she had another attack—if she fell——'

'I do appreciate the situation, Doctor,' said Abby unhappily, 'but I don't see what I can do.'

'Contact her,' he begged. 'Try and persuade her that my efforts are for her own good. She might listen to you.'

Abby shook her head. 'And she might not.'

'But you will try?'

'Of course.' Abby hesitated. 'She's not in any danger, is she?'

'Only from her own stubbornness,' retorted Dr Willis shortly. 'I'll leave it with you, Mrs Roth. Do your best.'

The problem of what to do about Aunt Hannah occupied the rest of the day, but by the evening Abby had come to a tentative conclusion. She would have to go to Rothside. She could not trust this to a letter, and perhaps it was time she stopped running away from the past.

A telephone call to British Rail solicited the information that there were frequent inter-city services between King's Cross and Newcastle, and from there it should be possible to take a bus to Alnbury. It was a long way to go, just for a weekend, and there was always the chance of hold-ups, but it would have to be done. She would never forgive herself if anything happened to Aunt Hannah, and she had done nothing to help.

She refused to consider what she would do if she met Piers. There was no earthly reason why they should meet. She was only going to be in Rothside for forty-eight hours. And besides, why should she be apprehensive? The divorce was only a formality, as he had said. They had had no communication for almost twelve years. They were strangers. She doubted he would even recognise her.

She arrived back at the flat, mentally planning what she ought to take with her. Matthew was in from school, she saw with relief, watching television in the living room.

Her words of greeting were answered by a grunt, and she unloaded her shopping in the kitchen before telling him of her arrangements.

'You remember what I was telling you about Aunt Hannah?' she ventured, when the fish fingers she had brought in for their tea were browning under the grill. 'About her having a heart attack?'

'Hmm.' Matthew was engrossed in the antics of the latest group of cartoon detectives, and was only paying her scant attention.

'Matthew!' Abby spoke his name a little impatiently, and he glanced round.

'I'm listening.'

'Well——' She paused a moment to marshall her words. 'I thought we might go up to Rothside this weekend to see her.'

'Hmm—*what?*' At last she had his interest. 'You mean—go to Northumberland?'

'To Rothside, yes.'

'Blimey!' Matthew gazed up at her with the first trace of genuine enthusiasm she had seen for ages. 'Do you mean it?'

'Yes,' Abby nodded, a little surprised at his reaction. She had half expected him to complain because it meant he would miss the first home game of the new football season.

'Hey!' Matthew actually grinned. 'Terrific!'

Abby shook her head. 'You don't mind.'

'Mind?' He snorted. 'Will we get one of those high-speed trains? You know, the ones that do over a hundred miles an hour?'

'Perhaps.' Abby was relieved. 'Then we have to take a bus from Newcastle to Alnbury.'

'Alnbury? Where's that?'

'Oh, it's about five miles from the village. It's where I used to go to school.' She broke off abruptly. 'Set the table, will you, Matt? The fish fingers smell as if they're burning.'

Abby booked seats on the five-forty p.m. train to

Newcastle on Friday evening. She arranged to pick
Matthew up from school at four o'clock, which gave them
plenty of time to get from Greenwich, across London to
King's Cross.

'Try and keep yourself clean,' she requested urgently,
when he went off to school on Friday morning in his best
trousers and school blazer, and Matthew grimaced good-
naturedly, content for once to wear his uniform. He really
had been remarkably good since he learned about the
trip, Abby reflected, as she rode the bus to work. Perhaps
he had decided to turn over a new leaf, she thought, but
she wasn't optimistic.

Her own boss, Trevor Bourne, had agreed to her leaving
early without objection. 'I just wish it was a job interview
you were attending, Abby,' he declared ruefully. 'I know
how much your independence means to you, don't I?'

Abby smiled. 'If you mean what I think you mean,
then yes, my independence is important to me,' she
averred firmly. 'It wouldn't work, Trevor. You've been a
bachelor too long.'

To her relief, Trevor let it go at that. Periodically, he
tried to introduce a more personal note to their relationship, but so far Abby had resisted his attempts. She
liked him. She liked working for him. But anything else
was totally unacceptable. It wasn't that she was frigid.
On the contrary, there were times when the underlying
needs of her own body drove her to consider any alter-
native. But there was always Matthew to apply the brake,
Matthew's opinion of her to care about, and the reluctant
betrayal of her own self-respect if she indulged in a merely
physical assuagement.

Matthew was waiting for her when she arrived at his
comprehensive school a few minutes after four. His blazer
was a little dusty, as if it had suffered from contact with
the tarmaced playground, but at least the day was fine,
and there was no mud to worry about. His boots she was
less impressed with. But the only shoes he possessed were
track shoes, and as he had refused to consider regular
schoolwear, she had been obliged to humour him.

Now he took the suitcase she was carrying from her as they hurried to catch the bus, and Abby knew an unexpected feeling of being cared for. Matthew could be so sweet when he chose, she thought, giving him a warm smile as he took his seat beside her. If only he chose more often, how much easier her life would be.

The train left on time. It was full of business men, returning to the north after a day's outing in London. Briefcases were the order of the day, and there was plenty of room for their bags and belongings between the seats.

Dinner was served on the train, but Abby had brought sandwiches, and Matthew munched happily as they plunged through the rolling downs surrounding London, and on to the flatter countryside bordering East Anglia. It was still light as they swept through Peterborough and Grantham, but by the time they reached their first stopping place at York, lights were springing up around the train, and dusk had deepened the shadows.

Matthew was growing restless now. With their meal over, and over an hour still ahead of them, he asked if he could go for a walk along the train, and realising she was as nervous as he was, she let him go.

In his absence, she pulled out her compact and examined her pale features with some trepidation. Had she changed so much? she asked herself anxiously. Twelve years was a long time. She was no longer eighteen, she was almost thirty, and the innocence of youth had given way to a guarded experience. She was different in ways that a mirror could not reveal. Although her eyes were still green between smoky lashes, they seemed to have lost their sparkle, and she was probably lucky her hair was that streaky shade of ash blonde. At least no one could see the grey hairs that must be there among the silver strands. Her skin was still good, and she seldom wore a lot of make-up, but nothing could alter the fact that she was a woman now, not a girl, and certainly not the girl who had married Piers Roth.

Matthew came back, his lean face glowing in the dim light. On occasions like this, she thought he did resemble his father, but mostly he took after her, with his fair hair and pale colouring. 'I opened the window on the door and looked out for a bit,' he explained, appalling her anew by his casual announcement. They could have passed a signal box, a bridge, anything, and the terrifying pictures these images created caused her to shake her head in horror. 'It's okay,' he added, noticing her reaction. 'I didn't do anything dangerous. I just wanted to see the engine, but the door into the driver's section was locked.'

'Oh, Matt!' Abby gazed at him in helpless fascination, and he shrugged his wide shoulders.

'Well . . .' he grimaced, 'I've never been on a diesel train before, and I wanted to get to know all about it, so I could tell the guys.'

'The *guys*!' Abby shook her head. 'Don't you mean— the boys?'

Matthew grinned. 'Okay, the *boys*,' he mimicked her humorously, and she thought again how likeable he was when he wasn't continually trying to score points.

'You look pale,' he continued, surveying her with steady consideration. 'You're not still worrying about Aunt Hannah, are you?'

'Well, I am worried, of course, but I didn't realise it showed so badly,' she responded dryly. 'What's the matter? Do I look a hag? I must admit, I've been wondering if she'll recognise me.'

'Why?'

'Why?' Abby shook her head. 'It is ten years since she's seen me, Matt.'

'So what? You don't look old.'

'Thank you.'

'As a matter of fact, one of the fifth-formers asked if you were my sister the other day,' he told her, with some reluctance. 'I said you were my mother, and he said you must have been a schoolgirl when you had me. I socked him!'

'Oh, Matt!' Abby was disturbed, but touched that he should care what people said of her.

'Well . . .' Matt hunched his shoulders, 'he was implying I didn't have a father. Rotten bastard!'

'Matt!' Abby's lips parted. 'Don't ever let me hear you use that word again!'

'Well, it's true. Nobody believes me when I say my parents are separated. They think you were never married.'

'But you and I know, Matt.'

'Do we?' Momentarily, his expression darkened, but then, as if determined not to let what other people thought cloud his enjoyment of the trip, he forced a smile and glanced out the window. 'Where are we? Is this Newcastle?'

Taking her cue from him, Abby forced her own sense of apprehension aside, and looked about her. 'No, this is Darlington,' she said, as they slowed to approach the station. 'Then there's Durham, and after that, Newcastle.'

'Good.' Matthew rested his elbows on the table in front of him and watched the activity on the platform. 'What time will we get to Alnbury? Does Aunt Hannah know we're coming?'

'I hope so.' Abby answered his second question first. 'I wrote to her yesterday, so she should have received the letter this morning. I would have sent a telegram, but I was afraid she might be alarmed at its arrival. Old people are funny. They associate telegrams with bad news.' She sighed. 'We received a telegram when my father was drowned.'

'Grandfather Charlton?'

'That's right,' Abby nodded reminiscently. 'Aunt Hannah was so kind to me. I'll never be able to repay her.'

Matthew was silent for a while, but then, as the train gathered speed again, he said: 'How will we get to Rothside? You said we could catch a bus to Alnbury.'

'Yes, we can.' Abby frowned. 'I'm not sure now where the bus station is, in relation to the railway station, I mean. But we can always ask someone. If we get into Newcastle on time, we should be able to catch the nine o'clock bus to Alnbury. That will get us there about ten.'

'Isn't that late for an old lady?' asked Matthew, with his usual pragmatism, and Abby had to concede that it was.

'Let's hope she appreciates the effort,' she said, with enforced lightness, but as the train neared Newcastle, her nerves were sharpening.

The train ran into the station at Newcastle at a little after ten minutes to nine, and by the time Abby had extracted them and their luggage, it was five to. The chances of them catching the nine o'clock bus were growing slimmer by the moment, and the idea of hanging about for another hour was daunting.

'Don't panic,' said Matthew, striding along the platform beside her, as she rummaged in her handbag for their tickets. 'There may be a bus at half past nine.'

'I'm sure there isn't——' Abby was beginning, only to break off abruptly at the sight of the man standing ahead of them at the barrier. Tall and lean, his thin dark face was unmistakable beneath hair that was more black than brown. He had changed. He was older, and perhaps a little broader, but she recognised him instantly, as if his image had been engraved in her thoughts.

She halted abruptly, and Matthew halted too, gazing at her impatiently. 'Mum——'

'Just a minute.' She made the excuse of searching through her bag to give herself more time, but nothing could alter the fact that he was there, and waiting for them.

Aunt Hannah shouldn't have done it, she thought frustratedly. She wasn't prepared, she wasn't ready. The last thing she had expected was to meet him tonight, and she looked at Matthew anxiously, wondering how he would react to this.

'What's wrong?' Matthew was looking at her strangely now, his fair brows drawing together as he identified her consternation. 'What is it? Don't you feel well? Mum, it's nearly nine o'clock. Don't you want to catch that bus?'

Abby's mouth opened and closed as she tried to find

words to explain what was about to happen. 'I—we—we may not need to catch the bus,' she began, glancing towards the barrier, and Matthew swung round curiously, perplexed as to her reasoning.

But even as Abby was trying to summon a stumbling explanation, something else happened, something that caused the hammering palpitation of her heart to pause sickeningly for a second, before racing unsteadily on. Piers was smiling at someone, speaking to someone who had emerged from the first class compartments of the train. And that someone was small and feminine, and, despite the mild September evening had a silky fur coat draped about her slim shoulders. Valerie Langton? Abby wondered, trying to control the giddy feeling of faintness that was sweeping over her, and Matthew looked from her to the barrier and then back at her again.

'What is it?' he demanded, as Abby endeavoured to keep her balance. 'Mum, what's going on? Is it that man? What's he doing here? Do you know him?'

Abby's tongue circled her parched lips. 'I—I thought I did,' she murmured, realising she had to pull herself together. 'My, it's warm tonight, isn't it?' She fanned herself nervously. 'I feel quite hot.'

'You don't look hot,' declared Matthew, transferring the suitcase and her holdall to one hand and putting the other through her arm. 'You don't have any colour at all,' he added, beginning to hustle her towards the ticket collector.

'Oh—wait!' The girl in the fur coat was still at the barrier, handing over her ticket, talking to Piers as she did so. 'I—there's no point in hurrying now, Matt. We won't catch that bus.'

'But you said something about us not needing to catch the bus,' he exclaimed, his suspicions fully aroused now. 'Mum, you do know that man, don't you? Who is it? My father?'

Abby wished she could have fainted then. It would have been so much easier just to collapse in a graceful heap and allow other people to take responsibility for what might happen. Even Matthew couldn't ignore her if she lost consciousness at his feet, and anything was better than having to run the risk of Piers turning and seeing her.

'*Mum!*' Matthew was speaking to her again, and helplessly she shook her head.

'All right,' she said, 'it is your father. But he hasn't come to meet us, as you can see.'

Matthew's expression revealed a conflicting number of emotions in quick succession, and then he turned to gaze at the man by the barrier with wide incredulous eyes.

Piers was moving away at last, Abby saw with relief. His companion had slipped her arm through his, and a porter had been engaged to carry her two suitcases. No doubt he had his car outside, she thought, trying not to feel bitter. No buses for Miss Langton. A comfortable ride home in the front of Piers' limousine. Of all the bad luck, she fretted—that Piers should be at the station, tonight of all nights. Poor Matthew! How must he be feeling? Seeing his own father for the first time, and not being able to identify himself!

She was handing over their tickets to be clipped when Matthew darted away from her. One moment he was there, standing beside her, holding their cases; the next, he had dropped the cases to the ground and was sprinting after Piers and the girl.

Abby's initial sense of horror froze any protest she might have made. It was like some awful nightmare. She was powerless to stop him, and with a dry mouth and quivering limbs she could only watch her son catch up with the other two. She saw him touch Piers's sleeve, she saw him speak to him; and she saw the look of dismay that crossed the girl's face as she looked incredulously up at the man beside her.

CHAPTER TWO

ABBY woke the next morning with a distinct feeling of disorientation. It was the silence that was the most disturbing aspect, the cessation of the sounds she had heard every morning for the past dozen years, and which generally awakened her before her alarm. Now there was no sound but the occasional cooing of the doves from the rooftop, and the argumentative chatter of starlings, quarrelling over the crumbs on the lawn.

She was at Rothside, she remembered with sudden apprehension. She was lying in her own bed at Ivy Cottage, the bed she had slept in for more than fifteen years, before Piers, and their marriage, had destroyed that life for ever.

Pushing back the bedcovers, she padded across the floor, her toes curling when they missed the rug and encountered the polished wood. Her window was set under the eaves, and she had to bend her head to look out of it, but the view that met her anxious gaze was as familiar as it had ever been.

Ivy Cottage was set on the outskirts of the village, but if she turned her head, she could see the green some yards away, and the duckpond, where she used to sail her paper boats. It was not a large village. Apart from the post office and general stores, there were no other shops, and in winter it was not unusual for them to be cut off for days, when the snow was heavy. But it was home to her, much more her home, she realised, than the flat in Greenwich could ever be, and she looked rather wistfully at the grey stone buildings. If only she had never married Piers Roth, she thought, she might still be living here. If, instead of marrying a man not only older, but whose way of life had been so much different from hers, she had married Tristan Oliver, none of this would have happened. She wondered, with a pang, how she might have adapted to being a farmer's wife. Certainly, Piers' mother would have said it was more appropriate. She had never wanted Abby to marry her son. She had opposed their relationship in every way she could, and only Piers' persistence had prevailed. But, as things had turned out, her fears had been vindicated, at least so far as the Roths were concerned.

Turning from the window, Abby wrapped her arms tightly about her thinly-clad body. She had not wanted to think about the Roths, but after what had happened the night before, she could think of little else. That scene at the station was imprinted on her mind in stark and humiliating detail, and the remembrance of Matthew's behaviour filled her with both anger and pity.

It had all been so awful—so embarrassing—so absurdly comical. Not that she had found any of it funny. On the contrary, she had wanted to die a thousand deaths when Piers turned and looked at her with that cold calculating stare. Yet in retrospect, it had had its moments of humour, if any of them had been objective enough to see them.

But none of them had, of course. Matthew's impulsive self-introduction had robbed the scene of any amusement, and Abby had the distinct impression that Piers thought she had put him up to it.

Oh, it had been terrible! Putting up her palms to her hot cheeks, Abby shuddered with revulsion, and unable to stand her own company any longer, she put on her dressing gown and made her way downstairs.

Although it was only half past seven, Hannah Caldwell was already up and dressed. For all her great age, she seemed hardly to have changed since Abby saw her last, though perhaps she moved a little slower as she took the kettle off the stove. She turned as her niece entered the kitchen and surveyed Abby with warm affection, indicating the cups on the tray and the teapot steaming beside it.

'I was just going to bring us both a pot of tea upstairs,' she declared, her rosy cheeks dimpling with pleasure. 'But now you're up, we can have it down here.'

Abby squeezed the hand the old lady offered, and went to sit at the kitchen table. She might never have been away, she reflected, blinking back a feeling of emotionalism. Thank heavens for Aunt Hannah, she thought, drawing a steadying breath. Right now, she needed someone to talk to.

'So . . .' The old lady set the tray between them, and seated herself opposite. 'You're here!' She reached for Abby's hand again. 'Are you going to stay?'

'Just for the weekend,' said Abby brightly, trying to behave naturally. 'You know that. I told you in my letter——'

'Yes, I know. But you also told me you were worried about Matthew, and now that I've met him, I can understand why.'

Abby sighed, and rested her chin on her knuckles. 'You mean what happened last night?'

'I mean the reasons behind what happened last night,' replied Hannah, pouring the tea. 'Abby, why haven't you told Matthew the truth?'

'How could I?' Abby cradled her cup in her cold hands. 'He'd never believe me. Not now.'

'What do you mean? Not now?'

Abby shook her head. 'It was easier to pretend his father was dead. I mean—so far as we were concerned, he was.'

'Oh, Abby!'

'Well . . .' Abby tried to justify herself. 'Aunt Hannah, Piers had disowned us; he'd disowned Matthew. Could you have told him that?'

'When did he find out?'

'About two years ago.'

'How?'

Abby hesitated. 'He—must have seen his birth certificate.'

'And?'

Abby put her cup down. 'He read one of your letters, while I was out.' She made a helpless gesture. 'It was my fault. I should have realised he was getting older, more inquisitive.'

'You mean he put two and two together.' Hannah sighed. 'I'm sorry, my dear, I should have been more careful.'

'Why should you?' Abby was quick to reassure her. 'I mean, you never used Piers' surname. But his christian name is rather—uncommon.'

'But you told Matthew the truth, then?'

'I told him that Piers and I were incompatible. That our marriage had been a mistake, and we had agreed to separate.'

'Is that all!' Hannah stared at her impatiently. 'Didn't you tell him about the rows? About Tristan?'

'Would that have made it any better?' Abby expelled her breath wearily. 'It was too late, don't you see? Any chance I had had of gaining Matt's sympathy was gone. He blamed me. He still does, as last night proved.'

'Oh, my dear!' Hannah looked concerned. 'Tell me again what happened. You were upset last night. And I didn't like to probe too deeply; not then.'

'Oh——' Abby flung herself back in her chair. 'It was awful!' She shook her head reminiscently. 'Matt had been so good, so—helpful. I really had begun to believe he'd turned over a new leaf. I had no idea he knew about Piers' letter and the divorce. If I had, I'd have thought twice about bringing him.'

Hannah nodded. 'Go on. You said you saw Piers at the barrier.'

'That's right. He'd come to meet Miss Langton. Apparently she'd been visiting some friends in London, and she happened to travel back on the same train. In first class, of course.'

'Of course.'

'Well——' Abby caught her lower lip between her teeth for a moment, 'when I saw Piers, I thought at first——' She broke off. 'I'm sure you can guess what I thought.'

'That I'd asked him to meet you?'

'Hmm,' Abby nodded. 'It was stupid, I realise that now. But at the time, it seemed the only explanation.'

'And you told Matthew?'

'Not then, no. But I was stunned, shocked; you can guess how I was feeling.' She lifted her shoulders helplessly. 'And Matt—being Matt—came to the obvious conclusion.'

'But why did you let him run after Piers? Surely you must have had some idea of what might happen.'

Abby sniffed. 'I didn't *let* him. I couldn't stop him. He was gone almost before I realised it.'

'And he introduced himself to Piers as his son.'

'Yes.' Abby felt the whole weight of this realisation bearing down on her.

'Still,' Hannah poured herself more tea, 'at least Piers didn't disown him in front of Miss Langton.'

'No.' Abby was grudging. 'But he didn't exactly welcome him either.'

'You couldn't expect that.' Hannah studied her niece's pale face with compassion. 'My dear, can you imagine what a shock it must have been for Valerie? No one in the valley even knew you had a son. And the Langtons regard Piers as one of them.'

Abby finished her tea and pushed her cup over for more. 'I suppose you're right. But at the time, all I was aware of was Piers looking at me as if he could have killed me!'

'Well, you've certainly put the cat among the pigeons, haven't you, my dear? I mean—an ex-wife is one thing, a stepson is something else.'

Abby shrugged. 'Piers doesn't regard Matt as his son. I expect he told Miss Langton that, the minute we got out of the car.'

'Well, at least you didn't have to wait for a bus,' pointed out Hannah dryly. 'Piers' Daimler must have been an improvement on that.'

'I suppose so.' Abby shuddered again. 'But it was the longest journey of my life. No one spoke, not even Matt. Perhaps he was regretting what he had done. Anyway, we all just sat there, like dummies, waiting to get to our destination.'

'Didn't Piers ask how you were? Why you were here?'

'Not in the car. I don't remember anything he said, just his hostility. It was awful!'

'And how did he introduce you to Valerie?'

'Oh—as his ex-wife, I think. It was humiliating. I think she thought Matt was some kind of punk!'

Hannah half smiled. 'Well, you have to admit, it's not every day a youth rushes up to your fiancé and claims that he's his father!'

'No.' Abby had to giggle at this. 'I suppose it was quite amusing really. I just wish it hadn't happened.'

'Never mind.' Hannah put the cups aside and regarded her warmly. 'You've no idea how good it is to have you here, Abby. The cottage has been so empty all these years.'

Abby allowed her to take both her hands, and they looked affectionately at one another. 'It's good to see you, too, Aunt Hannah,' she said gently. 'And what's all this about you misbehaving yourself?'

'Oh——' Hannah drew her hands away. 'You mean that conversation you had with Dr Willis. I told you in my letter, I have no intention of leaving the cottage. If I die, I intend to die here, and not in some home, with none of my own things around me.'

'I'm sure you're allowed to take your own things with you, Aunt Hannah,' Abby exclaimed. 'Your personal things, at least.'

'And my furniture? That dresser, for instance. Do you think I could take that? And my china cabinet, in the front parlour?'

'Aunt Hannah——'

'Don't bother. I know what you're going to say. I can't expect a residential establishment such as Rosemount to provide space for all the odds and ends its inmates have collected over the years.'

'You make it sound like a prison, Aunt Hannah!'

'It would be, to me. Abby, can't you see? Can't you understand? I've lived in this cottage almost all my life. I don't want to leave it now.'

'Then you'll have to have a nurse—or a housekeeper. Someone who could take care of you——'

'I don't want some strange woman in my kitchen,' the old lady interrupted her crisply. 'I don't want any female telling me what to do in my own home!'

'But, Aunt Hannah——'

'It's no good, Abby. My mind's made up. And if you've come up here to try and change it, you're wasting your time.'

Abby shook her head. 'Dr Willis says you shouldn't be alone.'

'Then you come home,' said Hannah flatly. 'There's no reason why you shouldn't, not now you and Piers are getting a divorce. Come back to Rothside. I'd employ you. And it would give Matthew the chance to get to know his real background.'

'I couldn't!' Abby was appalled.

'Why couldn't you? Oh, I know—because of your job in London. Well, I daresay I'd see you didn't lose by it.'

'It's not that.' Abby shook her head.

'No?' Hannah frowned. 'You're tired of working in London?'

'No.' Abby hesitated. 'As a matter of fact, Bourne Electronics is going out of business.'

'It is?' Hannah looked delighted. 'There you are, then. Your problems are solved.'

'No, Aunt Hannah.'

'Why not?'

Abby bent her head. 'The Roths wouldn't like it, you know they wouldn't.'

Hannah snorted. 'So what? Since when do I care what the Roths think?'

'Oh, Aunt Hannah!' Abby gazed at the old lady helplessly. 'I couldn't do that to Piers.'

'Do what?' Hannah looked impatient. 'Living in the south has made you soft, girl! Have you forgotten what Piers did to you? Is Matthew Piers' son or isn't he?'

'You know he is.'

'There you are, then.' Hannah's gnarled fingers

clenched. 'Don't you think it's about time he faced the truth? He's got away with it long enough.'

'I want nothing from him, Aunt Hannah,' said Abby quickly.

'All right.' Hannah shrugged. 'I'd be the last person to try and persuade you. But you're letting him have it all his own way, can't you see that? Where's your fighting spirit, girl? What have you got to lose?'

'I couldn't do it.' Abby got up from the table and moved to the window, looking out on the patch of garden at the back of the house. It was sadly neglected now. Where once she remembered a vegetable and flower garden, now there was only grass and weeds, choking the struggling rose bushes, that had survived in spite of everything. Obviously, Aunt Hannah was too old to bend her back to the soil, and Abby, who had badly missed having a garden when she first moved into the flat, wished she had more time.

Hannah, too, got up from the table now, and evidently abandoning her efforts to persuade her, said: 'What will that young man upstairs want for breakfast? I've got eggs, and some home-cured bacon, and there's plenty of bread and butter.'

'Oh,' Abby turned, 'I'm sure some toast and marmalade would be fine.' She forced a smile. 'I'd better go and get dressed.'

Hannah nodded. 'Very well. And what about you? Don't tell me you don't eat breakfast.'

'Well, I don't, usually,' Abby admitted, and then, seeing Aunt Hannah's impatient expression, she added: 'But I will have some toast, too. If that's all right.'

'Toast!' snorted the old lady, fetching a loaf of crusty bread from the larder. 'A plate of ham and eggs would put a bit of flesh on you. You're nothing but skin and bone, do you know that?'

Abby shook her head goodnaturedly and started up the stairs. The winding cottage stairs opened off the kitchen, with a door set squarely at the bottom to keep out draughts. The cottage had once boasted three bedrooms, but when Abby first came to live with **Aunt Hannah**, she had had one of the larger bedrooms converted into a tiny bathroom and a boxroom, and it was the boxroom that Matthew was occupying now.

Matthew was still asleep when she peeped into his room, his head buried half under the covers. Obviously the trauma of meeting his father the night before did not weigh as heavily on his mind as it did on his mother's, and Abby closed the door again and left him.

The water was still cold in the tank, and she had to be satisfied with a chilly wash, before dressing in a cream shirt, made of a synthetic fibre that felt like silk, and a pair of jeans. She brushed her shoulder-length straight hair until it shone, and curved into her nape, and then went downstairs again, without troubling to put on any make-up.

Aunt Hannah had lit the fire in the kitchen grate now. 'To heat the water,' she explained, as Abby flicked a glance at the promising blue sky beyond the windows. 'Now are you sure I can't persuade you to have a nice boiled egg?'

Abby smiled. 'You've twisted my arm,' she said. 'All right, I'll have a boiled egg. Providing you'll join me.'

'Good.'

But as Hannah turned to take a pan from its hook beside the stove, a sudden knocking arrested her. Someone was at the back door, and Abby raised her brows enquiringly as Hannah wiped her hands on her apron.

'Probably the boy from the farm, wanting to know if I need any more eggs,' Hannah declared, crossing the room, and then fell back in surprise at the sight of her visitor. 'Piers!' she exclaimed, causing every inch of Abby's skin to prickle alarmingly. 'Why, come in, come in! You're an early riser.'

'When I have to be,' Piers remarked, stepping into the small kitchen and immediately dwarfing its size. 'Good morning, Abby. I see you're an early riser, too.'

Abby remained where she was, sitting by the table. She didn't altogether trust her legs if she was to try and rise, but that didn't prevent her from looking at Piers, and renewing the memories awakened the night before.

He seemed to have changed little, except, as she had thought, his shoulders were a little broader. Yet, for all that, his lean athletic frame seemed to show no trace of superfluous flesh, his clothes fitting him as well as they had ever done, and with a closeness that accentuated the powerful muscles beneath the cloth. His hair was shorter than it used to be, though it still brushed his collar at the back, flat and smooth, and as dark as a raven's wing. His face was harder, his eyes deeper set but just as unusual, their tawny brilliance guarding his expression. His nose was strong and prominent, his cheekbones high and narrow, his mouth at present straight and uncompromising, revealing nothing of the sensuality, he had once shown her. At thirty-seven, Piers Roth was, if anything, more attractive than he had been at twenty-three when Abby had first gone to work for him, and it crossed her mind how unfair it was that he should have evaded his responsibilities for so long.

When Abby did not answer him, Piers turned to Hannah, who was closing the door, and gave her one of his polite smiles.

'As you've probably guessed, Miss Caldwell, I've come to see Abby. Would you mind if I had a few words with her—alone?'

'Not at all.' Hannah looked to Abby for confirmation. 'You can use the parlour. You'll be private enough in there.'

Abby was tempted to **refuse** to speak to him, after his silence the night before, but meeting Aunt Hannah's eyes, she knew she could not cause a scene without upsetting the old lady.

Getting up from her chair, she glanced at Piers, indicating that he should follow her, and opening the door into the tiny hall, led the way into the front parlour.

It was a chilly room, despite the strengthening warmth outside. The parlour faced north, and seldom got any sun, and in consequence it had an air of dampness and neglect.

Like the garden, thought Abby inconsequently, trying not to let the prospect of the coming interview unnerve her.

She hung back to allow Piers to enter the room, but he stood politely aside until she had preceded him. Crossing the patterned carpet to the hearth, Abby shivered, not entirely because of the cold, and faced him rather defensively, her arms wrapped protectively across her body.

Piers closed the door behind him, and leaning back against the panels, surveyed the old-fashioned little room. An upright sofa and chairs, lots of little tables, and knick-knacks everywhere, it was typical of any Victorian parlour, and Abby wondered what he was thinking as he looked about him. Was he remembering the first time he had entered this room, the night Aunt Hannah had spent in Carlisle, visiting a sick cousin? Or was he recalling how they had once made love on the hearth, long after Aunt Hannah had gone to bed? The room had memories, memories she would rather forget, and she shifted a little uncomfortably as his eyes returned to her.

'You know why I'm here, of course,' he said, all trace of affability wiped from his voice. 'Perhaps you'd like to tell me what that little scene last night was meant to achieve. How did you know I'd be meeting that train? Did Hannah tell you? If so, I'd be interested to know where she got her information.'

Abby drew a deep breath, realising she would gain nothing by losing her temper. 'Believe it or not, you were the last person I expected to see. Or wanted to see, for that matter. As you know, Aunt Hannah's been ill. Her doctor asked me to try and persuade her how dangerous it is for her to live alone. That's the only reason I'm here.'

Piers' eyes were narrowed, the thick lashes she had once teased him were like a girl's, shadowing their expression. 'Wouldn't a letter have been just as effective—and less expensive?'

'Perhaps. But I happen to care about Aunt Hannah. She's the only person who's ever cared about me.'

A spasm of impatience crossed his face at her words, but he did not refer to them when he said: 'Why did you bring the boy with you? What useful purpose does he serve?'

Abby caught her breath. 'He's my son, Piers. And it may come as something of a shock to you to learn that I care about him, too.'

Piers straightened away from the door. 'Was there no one you could have left him with? A—friend, perhaps.'

Abby's resentment stirred. 'If you mean a *man* friend, then I'm afraid I must disappoint you. Matt and I live alone.'

Piers shrugged. 'Surely you have girl friends.'

'That's my affair.' Abby was getting annoyed, in spite of herself. 'And why shouldn't I bring Matt here? This is where he belongs.'

Piers' eyes were harsh with contempt. 'So that's what you've told him.'

Abby gasped, 'I haven't told him anything!'

'You told him that I was his father.'

'You are!'

Piers' lips curled. 'Oh, please! Let's not get into that again.' He breathed heavily. 'The fact remains, you told him who I was, you pointed me out. Why else did he come chasing after me, and subject both myself and Val to that embarrassing introduction?'

'It wasn't like that.' Abby was having difficulty now in keeping her temper in check. He was so sure of himself, so arrogant. And she could not deny the little spurt of irritation she had experienced when he spoke of the other girl in that possessive way. 'I got a shock,' she continued. 'It was—so unexpected. I didn't tell Matt who you were— not in so many words. I didn't have to. He guessed. And how could I anticipate what he would do?'

Piers thrust his hands into the pockets of the worn black corded jacket he was wearing. 'You're telling me he saw a complete stranger and guessed I was his father?' he demanded caustically. 'Credit me with a little intelligence, Abby, please.'

'You—bastard!' Abby gazed across at him bitterly. 'Do you think I wanted him to know his own father had disowned him? Do you think I'd have let him take the risk that you might deny all knowledge of him?' She shook her head. 'Until two years ago, he thought you were dead! I wish he still believed it.'

Piers regarded her sceptically. 'What are you saying? That he suddenly discovered we were related?'

'He read a letter Aunt Hannah sent me,' declared Abby tersely. 'He saw your name in it and identified it as being the same as that on his birth certificate. He's not stupid, you know. The chances of my knowing two men called Piers are rather remote, don't you think?'

Piers' mouth compressed. 'So you told him your story.'

'No!' Abby was indignant. 'I didn't tell him any story. I simply explained that—that our marriage hadn't worked. That we were—incompatible.'

'And I suppose there's no connection between my writing to you about the divorce and your turning up here.'

'No!' Abby was adamant.

Piers made a sound midway between acknowledgement and derision, and then walked broodingly across to the leaded windows. Beyond Aunt Hannah's small patch of garden, a sleek Mercedes station wagon was parked in the road. Grey, with an elegant red line along the side, it gleamed in the early morning light, the sun glinting off polished metalwork and mirror-like chrome. Another of the estate vehicles, thought Abby, wishing he would go. The Roths spent more on cars every year than she and Matthew had to live on.

'What does the boy know about me?' Piers asked suddenly, keeping his back to her. 'I suppose he believes I'm to blame for the—what was it you said—the incompatibility of our marriage.'

'As a matter of fact, Matt blames me,' Abby flung at him angrily. 'That should please you. The ultimate irony!'

Piers turned. 'It doesn't please me at all,' he replied harshly. 'The boy's yours. Why don't you tell him the truth? That although he bears my name, he's not my son!'

'Because it wouldn't be true,' retorted Abby bleakly. 'Oh, why don't you go away, Piers? You're not wanted here. Don't worry, I'll see that Matt doesn't bother you again. We'll be leaving tomorrow.'

'Will you?' Piers walked back to his previous position, only nearer now, so that she could smell the warmth of his body, and the distinctive scent of the cheroots he evidently still favoured. Then he sighed before saying quietly: 'I believe you when you say you didn't expect to see me at the station.' He paused to give his words emphasis before continuing: 'I suggest it was an unfortunate incident, and that we both try and forget what happened.'

If he had expected his mild words would appease Abby, he was mistaken. On the contrary, she preferred it better when he was saying what he really thought, not paying lip service to a dead, or dying, relationship.

'How considerate of you!' she exclaimed tautly, too conscious of his nearness and resentful of her own reactions to it. 'Don't patronise me, Piers. I don't need it. Go, make your apologies to Miss Langton. She needs them—I don't.'

'I was not apologising!' Piers' tawny eyes glittered, hard and predatory, like a cat's. 'While I'm prepared to accept that you couldn't have known I was meeting Val off the train, I still say it was the height of folly to bring the boy up here, particularly at this time, knowing he was bound to be curious about me.'

'At this time?' Abby plucked the words out of his mouth. 'What do you mean, at this time?'

'I mean with the divorce pending.'

'Matt knows nothing about the divorce.'

'Are you sure?'

Piers was staring at her, and belatedly Abby wondered whether he might not be right. Apart from his initial enquiry, Matthew had showed no further interest in that other letter, and only now did she wonder whether, like Aunt Hannah's letter previously, he had found his father's communication and read it.

Now she shook her head a little uneasily, unable either

to deny or confirm his suspicions. 'I don't think he knows,' she said finally. 'But even if he does, what difference does it make?'

'You ask me that!' Piers drew a deep breath. 'For God's sake, Abby, the boy believes that I'm his father!'

'So?'

'God!' With a groan of anguish, Piers thrust the long fingers of one hand through his hair. 'Don't you understand? It doesn't matter what you or I believe. It's what he believes that counts. Do you want him to get hurt?'

'Why should you care?'

'I'd care about any child in similar circumstances.' Piers moved his shoulders impatiently. 'Abby, you've got to tell him the truth. The boy's bright enough. He'll understand.'

Abby's control snapped. 'Is that what you think? Is that what you really think?' Her green eyes darted fire. 'You supercilious prig! How dare you come here and preach to me about the son whose existence you've ignored for nearly twelve years! What do you care whether he's hurt or not? What feelings of remorse will you feel when Matthew and I are safely out of your life for good? How convenient it was to pretend Matthew wasn't yours! What a comfortable let-out, from a marriage gone sour! Why, you didn't even have to pay me any maintenance. You could forget all about us!'

Piers' jaw hardened. 'That's not true. I sent you money——'

'And I returned it,' cut in Abby contemptuously. 'I didn't want your charity!'

'It was not charity.'

'What was it, then?' Abby found she was actually enjoying his evident frustration. 'A bid to salve your conscience?' she taunted. 'An attempt to prove that all I really wanted was your money? Or a way to appease those feelings of guilt you couldn't quite erase?'

'No!' With a face contorted by the strength of his emotions, Piers' hand came out and closed about her upper arm, jerking her towards him. 'Believe it or not, one of us still possessed some sense of decency,' he snapped, his fingers digging into her flesh. 'You selfish little bitch! When did you ever think of anyone else but yourself?'

Abby brought her hand back then and slapped him, the sound of the impact ringing round the cluttered little room. It was an instinctive reaction to what he had said, an uncontrollable impulse that she regretted almost as soon as it was done. With a sense of horror, she watched the white marks her fingers had made appear on his cheek, and sensed the iron control he was exerting not to respond in kind.

'I should have expected that from you,' he grated, and for a few agonising seconds, Abby thought he was about to exact revenge. His grip on her arm tightened, and she was forced even nearer, so that she could feel the hard muscles of his thigh against her hip.

With an unsteady gaze she looked up at him, close enough now to see the pulse beating at his jawline, the flaring hollows of his nostrils, and the thick curling lashes with their sun-bleached tips. He was breathing heavily, his narrow lips separated to reveal the even whiteness of his teeth, his breath mingling with hers, warm and sweet. But it was the savage brilliance of his eyes that held her gaze, those strange tawny irises, flecked with gold, and undoubtedly smouldering with the heat of his anger. They impaled her like a sword, hard and unyielding, and filled with—contempt?

She wasn't sure any more. As he continued to hold her, as the warmth of her body against his thigh penetrated the fine cloth of his trousers, his expression changed, became fiercer and yet more malleable, his unwilling awareness of her as a woman superseding the violent revulsion she provoked.

'I should kill you!' he muttered, bending his head towards her, and Abby's quivering lips parted almost involuntarily.

He was going to kiss her, she thought incredulously. In spite of his contempt, his anger, his *hatred*, he still had some feeling for her, and her limbs turned to water as his passionate gaze swept down to her mouth.

And then she was free. In the space of a moment, her blind anticipation of his touch became an unforgivable weakness, and she despised herself utterly as he strode towards the door.

He turned as he reached the door, and with his fingers on the handle, regarded her contemptuously. 'I hope I never have to see you again,' he said, any emotion she imagined she had seen in his face erased completely. 'You're right—I was glad of the child's birth to escape from an impossible relationship. Our marriage was a farce from the beginning. Perhaps I should have told you the truth before I married you. Perhaps I was to blame for that. But how was I to know then what an over-sexed little bitch you were, and how little time it would take before you betrayed yourself!'

CHAPTER THREE

'MUM?'

Matthew's anxious voice from the open doorway alerted her to the fact that she was no longer alone. It took quite an effort to turn and face him, aware as she was that her eyelids were probably puffy, and the evidence of her recent bout of weeping was impossible to hide. But he had to be answered, and she held her handkerchief to her nose as she turned about.

'You're up,' she said, unnecessarily, mentally noting the fact that his jeans were getting too short for him again. 'I—did you sleep well? I expect Aunt Hannah will give you some breakfast if you ask her.'

'She's boiling me two eggs,' said Matthew, shifting his weight from one foot to the other. 'What's the matter, Mum? Why have you been crying?'

Abby sighed, and put her handkerchief away. 'Oh—you know how it is,' she murmured, hoping to divert him. 'Old places, old memories——'

'My father's been here, hasn't he?' Matthew stated flatly, shocking her out of her lethargy. 'I heard his voice. It woke me up. Why did he come here so early?'

Abby struggled to find an answer for him. 'Your—your father's a busy man,' she got out at last. 'I expect he has things to do later.'

'It was about last night, wasn't it?' mumbled Matthew, scuffing his toe. 'He was annoyed because I broke in on his meeting with that Langton woman.'

'Well, you did embarrass him,' agreed Abby wearily. 'Matt, let's not go over that again now. You—you behaved impulsively, you didn't think what you were doing. I'm sure your father appreciates that. Let's forget it, shall we?'

'Forget it!' Matthew's jaw jutted. 'I don't want to forget

it. At least I've met him now. And I think he liked
me. 'Course, with that silly female being there, we
couldn't have a proper conversation, but when I see him
again——'

'Again!' Abby stared at him. 'Matt, you won't be seeing
him again.'

'Why not?' Matthew's mouth took on a downward
slant. 'You can't stop me from seeing him. He's my father.
Why do you think I was so keen to come here? After
reading his letter, I knew it might be the last chance I'd
get.'

'You read your father's letter?'

Matthew had the grace to look a little shamefaced now,
but he bluffed it out. 'Why shouldn't I?' he demanded.
'You weren't going to tell me, were you? He wants a
divorce—I read that. Why? Does he want to marry that
Langton woman?'

'Oh, Matt!' Abby shook her head helplessly. 'I wish
you'd try to understand. Your—your father isn't interested in us, in *either* of us. He just wants his freedom.'

Matthew looked sulky. 'You don't know that. You think
because he doesn't want you, it follows that he doesn't
want me. Well, that needn't be true. Lots of couples
separate, but the kids get to see both parents—regularly.'

'It's not like that.' Abby was close to telling him exactly
how it really was, but compassion forbade her from destroying what little dignity he had left. 'Matt, don't look
at me like that. It's not my fault, honestly. But—but
this morning your father told me that he doesn't want to
see—either of us again.'

'That's not true!'

'It is true.' Abby would have gone to him then and put
her hands on his shoulders, but Matt backed away.

'What did you say to him?' he demanded, and she was
dismayed to hear the choke of a sob in his voice. 'I bet
you told him to get lost. My father wouldn't refuse to see
me—he wouldn't! You've done this. It's all your fault.'

'Matt——'

But Matthew had gone, charging back through the kitchen as if the devil himself was at his heels. Abby followed him more slowly, hearing, like the death knell of all her hopes for their relationship, his booted feet hammering up the wooden staircase.

Hannah looked up from the bread she was cutting when Abby appeared, turning her head towards the stairs before giving the girl her attention. 'Whatever has happened?' she exclaimed. 'First Piers goes striding out of the house, without even a word of farewell, and now Matthew dashes up the stairs, as if you'd taken a whip to him!'

'Don't ask,' said Abby tiredly, sinking down into a chair beside the table. 'Honestly, sometimes I wish I'd died in childbirth, like my mother. I just don't think I've got the will to go on.'

'Of course you have.' Hannah spoke half angrily. 'And don't let me hear you suggest such a dreadful thing again! Be thankful for what you do have—your youth and your health. There's many a one would envy you, just remember that.'

Abby sighed. 'I know, I know. But I don't know what I'm going to do, Aunt Hannah. Matt blames me for everything. He even blames me for sending Piers away this morning, and goodness knows, that wasn't how it was.'

'Hah!' Hannah snorted impatiently. 'I suppose Piers came to tell you to keep the boy out of his way.'

'Something like that.'

Hannah shook her head. 'The man's a fool! Can't he see the resemblance between them? Both so stubborn! Both blaming you for something that wasn't your fault. I could knock their heads together!'

'If only it was that simple,' sighed Abby wryly. 'You know, I really believed that sooner or later Piers would begin to have doubts.'

'I doubt his mother would have let him,' retorted Hannah crisply, taking Matthew's eggs out of the pan. 'You really reinforced her position when you became pregnant so soon after your marriage. And she's had years to brainwash Piers into believing that story about you and Tristan.'

'I suppose Tristan going away didn't help.'

'No.' Hannah conceded the point. 'And for a while, the Olivers were very bitter. But Lucy's grown up now. Do you remember Lucy Oliver? Well, she's grown up and married, and her husband's taken over the running of the farm.'

'Tristan went to Canada, didn't he?'

'Yes,' Hannah nodded. 'And I believe he's done very well. He's married, too, of course—a Canadian girl, naturally. They have three children.'

'Lucky Tristan!' Abby gave a rueful sigh. 'How much simpler it would have been if I'd married Tristan when I had the chance.'

'You didn't love him,' declared Hannah practically. 'You think it would have been simpler, and perhaps it would, in some ways. But Abby, do you honestly think you'd have been happy, over a prolonged period? All right, so things with Piers didn't work out as you expected. At least you took your happiness while you had the chance.'

'For which I'm paying now,' remarked Abby dryly, putting up both hands to massage the aching muscles at the back of her neck. She moved her shoulders helplessly. 'Why couldn't Piers at least have given me an opportunity to explain? Or if he had agreed to speak to Dr Morrison again, taken some more tests——'

'Abby, Abby . . .' Hannah gazed at her compassionately. 'You really can't be that naïve! Not after more than twelve years of marriage. You know how important these things can be; particularly to a man. Piers had taken that medical, on his mother's advice, to assure himself that there was nothing wrong——'

'But the tests must have been wrong, you know that!' Abby exclaimed, blinking back the tears that persistently pricked at the backs of her eyes.

'Maybe.' Hannah acknowledged her words. 'But the fact remains that Piers had no reason to doubt their veracity. Surely now you realise how he must have felt. Good heavens, he didn't even tell you, even though that had been his mother's intention all along.'

'But she couldn't have believed that it would make any difference to my feelings for Piers!' Abby was incredulous.

'Why not? Most young women want children, even today.'

'But we could have adopted a child.'

'It's not the same. Or at least, Piers didn't think so. Abby, try to put yourself in his position. How would you have felt if some doctor had told you you couldn't have children?'

Abby shifted in her seat. 'Nevertheless, he should have given me a chance to explain——'

'I suppose he should. But the evidence was pretty damning, wasn't it? And then your discovering you were pregnant only weeks later.'

'Aunt Hannah!' Abby gazed indignantly at her aunt. 'Whose side are you on?'

'I'm only playing devil's advocate,' replied Hannah smoothly. 'I sympathise with you, my dear, you know I do. But I can't help thinking that running away didn't help anything.'

'I couldn't have stayed here.' Abby shuddered. 'I couldn't have had my baby here.'

'Why not?'

Abby shook her head. 'I didn't want Piers to see me. I didn't want him watching me, observing me—despising me when I grew fat and ugly——'

'Pregnant women do not grow fat and ugly,' exclaimed Hannah, impatiently. 'Stop exaggerating, Abby. You ran away because you hadn't the guts to stay and face them!'

'Aunt Hannah!'

'Well, it's true, Abby. I'm sorry, but it is. You've let the Roths determine how you live your life. Oh—going off to London may have been fine, and I'm not denying you've made a niche for yourself there. But don't imagine it was solely to prove your independence you left Rothside. You left because you let the Roths drive you away.'

Abby got up from the chair and walked unsteadily across to the windows. 'Is that what you really think of me?' she asked, in a small voice, and Hannah clicked her tongue before going after her and slipping her arm about her.

'My dear, you mean everything to me, you know that. But it's no use deluding yourself that by running away from a problem you can evade it. Sooner or later it always recoils on you, and I suggest that this is what's happened now.'

'With—with Matt, you mean?'

Hannah nodded.

'But what can I do?'

'Well, running away again isn't going to help.'

'What do you mean?' Abby turned to look at the old lady.

'Matthew isn't going to forgive you until you can prove to him that you were not to blame for what happened.'

'And how can I do that?'

'By coming back here to live. By giving him the chance to see his father as he really is.'

'No.' Abby moved her head vigorously from side to side. 'Aunt Hannah, I told you before, I couldn't do that.'

'Why couldn't you?'

'I told you. It wouldn't be fair.'

'To Piers?' Hannah made a sound of exasperation. 'Abby, Matthew is Piers' son!'

'I know.'

'Then what earthly right has he to be allowed to ignore the fact?'

Abby caught her lower lip between her teeth. 'What would people say? What would they think?'

'Does it matter? They'll probably think you had the child while you were in London. Which you did,' she added dryly, 'but you know what I mean.'

Abby hesitated. 'But how could I ever prove Matthew is Piers' son. He'll never believe me.'

'Perhaps *you* won't have to.'

'I don't understand.'

'Matthew,' said Hannah simply.

'Matthew?' Abby was confused.

'My dear, if you bring Matthew to live here, if you install him in the school at Alnbury, and you let him mix with the other boys from the village, can you imagine how Piers will feel?'

'I doubt he'll feel anything.'

'Won't he?' Hannah looked sceptical. 'Don't you think, human nature being what it is, he'll resent it.'

'Resent it, yes, but——'

'Listen to me, Abby. I'm a lot older and perhaps a little wiser than you are. All right, I agree that to begin with Piers will resent it, but give him time. Sooner or later, other emotions will take its place, and that's when his heart-searching will start.'

'Heart-searching!' Abby's lips twisted. 'Aunt Hannah, I think you're deluding yourself.'

'Remember, Abby, he's not going to be able to ignore you. Valerie Langton knows who you are, and thanks to Matthew, she knows who he is as well.'

'Do you think Piers will allow that to trouble him?' Abby expelled her breath heavily. 'Aunt Hannah, you know what Piers will have told her. The truth—as he sees it.'

'Nevertheless, the doubts have been planted.'

'Aunt Hannah, you're not being realistic.'

'No? The man loved you once, didn't he?'

' "Once" being the operative word.'

'Even so, seeing you again, hearing about you from other people in the village, as he's bound to do, is going to revive memories.'

'Memories he would rather forget.'

'Some of them, I agree. But there are others, Abby, that he won't find so easy to ignore.'

Abby moved away from her. 'Aunt Hannah, if you think, after all that has happened, I could ever forgive Piers for what he did——'

'I don't expect miracles,' retorted Hannah flatly. 'I

thought we were talking about Matthew. It's Matthew you should be thinking about, Matthew's future that should be ensured. He is Piers' son, Abby, and by rights the Manor estate should eventually come to him.'

'Well, yes, but——'

'At least give nature a chance. The boy is like his father. Oh, maybe it's not immediately obvious from his appearance. His colouring is yours, and just now, with that terrible haircut and those awful boots, he bears little resemblance to Piers at that age. But given time, and a change of environment, who knows what might happen? And I'd really like to see Piers' face when he begins to suspect he may have been wrong all these years.'

Abby's lips tightened. She would like to see that, too, she thought bitterly. Even if it wouldn't make any difference to what happened to her, it would be sweet revenge to know Piers was having to live with his folly for the rest of his life . . .

Matthew appeared at lunchtime. Hannah had taken his breakfast upstairs to him, and although she grimaced rather ruefully at Abby when she came downstairs again, when the tray was finally returned it had been cleared.

Abby was relieved to see her son and reassured to find he had apparently got over his distress. Apart from the faintly sullen expression in his eyes when he looked at her, he seemed much as usual, answering Aunt Hannah when she spoke to him, and making short work of the steak and kidney pie she had baked for lunch.

'Now, what are you going to do this afternoon?' Hannah asked, after Matthew had downed his second helping of apple crumble and was thirstily emptying a glass of lemonade. 'Abby?' she turned to her niece. 'Why don't you and Matthew go for a walk? I'm sure he'd like to look around the village.'

Abby met the old lady's innocent gaze with some frustration. Aunt Hannah didn't waste any time, she reflected wryly, knowing full well what her purpose was. She wanted Abby to talk to Matthew about moving to

Rothside. She wanted her to tell him of her suggestion that by doing so they would be serving the dual purpose of providing themselves with a permanent home and thus removing any necessity for Hannah to leave the cottage now or at some future date.

'I don't know,' Abby began, her eyes revealing her indecision, but Hannah was adamant.

'Go along with you,' she said. 'I'll do these dishes, and then put my feet up for half an hour. Dr Willis said I should rest every afternoon, and you know what these young doctors are like.'

'Matthew?' Abby turned to her son, half prepared for him to refuse her invitation, but he didn't.

'Why not?' he said, his eyes hard and insolent. 'If we're leaving tomorrow, I'd better make the best of it, hadn't I?'

Abby sighed, but she didn't argue with him. Instead, she told him to go and get ready, while she and Aunt Hannah cleared the table.

'I can do it,' Hannah exclaimed, when Abby insisted on installing her in the armchair by the fire, and started cleaning the plates.

'If you want me to stay, you're going to have to let me earn my keep,' retorted Abby dryly, and Hannah gazed at her disbelievingly as she turned back to the sink.

'Do you mean it?' she exclaimed, and Abby cast a rueful glance over her shoulder.

'If Matt's agreeable,' she conceded, resuming her task. 'I'm not making any promises, but as everything else seems to have failed, I'm prepared to give it a try.'

Abby tried to broach the subject with Matthew, as they left Ivy Cottage behind and walked along the grassy verge towards the village green. It was a beautiful afternoon, the air amazingly warm for so late in the summer, the bees buzzing among the wild flowers in the hedges. There was the smell of corn and new-mown hay, and the many indescribable scents of the country, the calls of the birds that swooped low over their heads mingling with the chatter of the ducks on the pond.

Matthew had been silent since they left the cottage, paying little attention to his surroundings as he kicked a pebble through the grass. Abby wondered whether he was aware of the beauty of his surroundings, or whether indeed such considerations ever occurred to him. He seemed sunk in some retrospection of his own, and judging by his expression, it was not to his liking.

'I used to sail paper boats on the pond when I was a little girl,' Abby ventured, hoping to arouse his interest, but Matthew's only reaction was a sideways glance. 'I was only three when I came to live with Aunt Hannah. I can't really remember Newcastle at all.'

Matthew did not respond, and pressing on, Abby pointed to a grey stone building, set back from the road. 'That's where I used to go to school, until I was old enough to attend the grammar school in Alnbury. They still had grammar schools in those days. Now I believe it's called Alnbury Comprehensive.'

There were some children playing on the green. A game of cricket was in progress, but they paused as Abby and Matthew walked by, no doubt wondering who they were, thought Abby tensely. She probably knew their parents, she reflected. Her generation were all married with families now, and none of these youngsters was older than Matthew.

At the far side of the green were the village stores and the post office, and beyond them, the grey spire of St Saviour's Church. It was the church where she and Piers had got married, and Abby avoided the adjoining rectory, half afraid the Reverend Mr Armstrong would appear and recognise her. It would be awkward introducing Matthew to him. As yet, she had not accustomed herself to the idea of telling everyone he was Piers' son, and she wondered if Aunt Hannah quite realised how awkward it was going to be. People might not believe her, and if Mrs Roth had her way, they definitely wouldn't. It was a formidable task she was setting herself, and she wondered rather apprehensively whether it was all worthwhile.

'Where does my father live?' asked Matthew suddenly,

startling her by the unexpectedness of his question, and she moistened her lips.

'Outside the village,' she said at last. 'He—well, he lives at Rothside Manor. The—er—the Roths gave Rothside its name.'

'I guessed that.' Matthew was insolent. 'So where is Rothside Manor?'

Abby hesitated. 'Why do you want to know?'

'Is it a secret?'

'No, it's not a secret, but I'd like you to answer.'

Matthew grimaced. 'Don't worry, I won't go trespassing on his property. I just want to know about him, about where he lives, about my grandparents.'

Abby's tongue circled her lips again. 'You don't have—grandparents. You have a grandmother—your father's mother, Mrs Roth.'

'What's she like?' Matthew was regarding her with evident interest, and Abby thought how ironic it was that Piers' mother should arouse such curiosity in the child she had done her utmost to destroy.

'I—why—she's all right,' she replied now, pushing her hands deep into the hip pockets of her jeans. 'Sixtyish, I suppose. The last time I saw her, she was very smart—grey-haired; enjoys riding, or she did. According to Aunt Hannah, she spends most of her time these days working for the good of the community. You know, church activities, charity functions. The kind of things you'd expect someone like her to do.'

'Are they rich?' Matthew was obviously intrigued, and his unnatural air of detachment receded as his interest was awakened. 'I suppose you used to live at the Manor, didn't you?' he added, after a moment's consideration. 'Did I live there, too?'

'No.' Abby felt her cheeks grow warm. 'Oh, look,' she said, walking on, 'isn't that a magpie?' She shook her head, as if it was the most important matter. 'You never see magpies in London.'

Matthew made no response, and she could tell by his hunched shoulders and the way he mooched after her that he was disappointed by her answer. Glancing his way, Abby wondered for the umpteenth time whether what she was about to do was the right thing for him, but if Aunt Hannah was correct, she had no right to deprive him of finding his real identity.

'Matt . . .'

She spoke quietly, but he must have heard her, for he lifted his head and fixed her with a resentful stare.

'Matt,' it was terribly difficult to know exactly how best to say this, but jumping in with both feet, she made her announcement: 'Aunt Hannah has suggested that perhaps we should come and—and stay with her for a while.'

Matthew's expression changed abruptly. 'Come and stay with her?' he echoed. 'What—do you mean for a holiday?'

'No.' Abby chose her words carefully. 'We would come and—and live here. For some time, anyway.'

'Live with Aunt Hannah?'

Matthew was looking uncertain now, and Abby pressed on: 'As you know, her doctor thinks she should not be living alone, not at her age, and with her heart not being strong. Actually, if you remember, you suggested something similar when we were at home—at the flat, I mean. You asked why Aunt Hannah couldn't come and live with us. Well, she's returned the compliment. She asked us to move instead.'

'Leave London?' Matthew was evidently trying to come to terms with this new development, and Abby nodded.

'It's not such a bad idea,' she added. 'I mean, what with me losing my job and everything. The flat was going to be very expensive for us to keep, and jobs aren't that easy to come by these days.'

Matthew frowned. 'Would we live at the cottage?'

'Of course.'

'It's not very big. Not for three people.'

'The flat isn't very big,' Abby pointed out equably. 'We'd manage.'

'Would I have to go to school up here?'

'Well, naturally.' Abby paused. 'You'd go to the comprehensive in Alnbury I was telling you about. I believe there's a school bus that picks up the children from all the outlying villages.' She forced a smile. 'In my day, we had to get the service bus.'

Matthew's mouth compressed. 'Did my father go to that school, too?' he asked suspiciously.

'No.' Abby sighed, then instilling a note of enthusiasm into her voice, she asked: 'What do you think? Shall we do as Aunt Hannah says?'

Matthew bent to pick a blade of grass, threading it through his teeth. Then, looking at her steadily, he said: 'Does my father know?'

Abby's cheeks flamed. 'No. Why should he? It's nothing to do with him what we decide to do.'

'This is his village, isn't it?'

'No!' Abby was appalled. 'The Roths may once have been the primary landowners around here, but time—and death duties—have changed all that. I'm not saying they're not comfortably off——'

'—and powerful,' inserted Matthew irritatingly, but she ignored him.

'They don't own Rothside, Matt. In fact, they don't mix with the local people much at all. Their friends mostly live outside the village.'

Matthew scowled. 'So how did you get to know my father?' he demanded, and Abby's doubts about this arrangement multiplied themselves.

'Do you really want to know?' she exclaimed. 'Matt, it's all in the past. It was a mistake. Do you really want to know about a mistake?'

'You mean I was a mistake,' he muttered resentfully, and Abby closed her eyes for a moment in bleak desperation.

'No,' she said at last, 'that's not what I meant. I meant our marriage was a mistake. Piers and I were from different backgrounds. It should never have happened. We had nothing in common.'

'Except me,' declared Matthew shrewdly.

'Matt, we split up before you were born!'

'Then maybe you shouldn't have,' he retorted aggressively. 'I should at least have been given the chance to choose which parent I wanted to live with.'

Abby gasped. Matthew had hurt her before, many times, but never as much as this, and she turned away helplessly, unable to say anything in the face of such brutal logic.

She had to steel herself to walk back to the cottage, and she was relieved to see Matthew had gone ahead. He had already reached the village green where the children were playing, and as he came abreast of the wicket, a tennis ball came bouncing across the road to roll to a stop at his feet.

Matthew bent and picked up the ball, and Abby was glad to see him joining in their game. If only he could become one of them, a normal healthy village child, it would be worth any heartache she might have to suffer.

One of the youngsters, a plump little boy, with a thatch of gingery hair, had gone up to Matthew and was obviously asking if they could have their ball back. Matthew towered above the small boy, the ball in his hands held well out of the child's reach. Abby, approaching them smiled at the boy before speaking to her son: 'Throw the ball back, Matt. You're holding up the game.'

Matthew hesitated, examining the ball in his hands as if looking for flaws. Then, without a word, he hurled it across the green, past the group of waiting children, and into the pond with a loud plop. The ducks all scattered, waddling out of the water, shaking their feathers and quacking in protest, and a smile of pure satisfaction spread over Matthew's face. 'Bullseye,' he remarked, brushing his hands together, and smirked at the little boy who was now very near to tears.

'You—you little beast!' Abby was trembling with reaction, as much from what he had said earlier as from this latest piece of badness. 'You're not fit to mix with decent children! Go back to the cottage and go to your room. I don't want to set eyes on you again until tomorrow!'

CHAPTER FOUR

FOR a moment, Abby thought Matthew was going to defy her. His face suffused with unbecoming colour, and his fists clenched at his sides, tight and muscular beneath the rigid thinness of his arms. But then, something—some spark of respect he still had for her perhaps, caused all the aggression to go out of him, and although his expression remained defiant, he slouched off towards the cottage.

Abby gathered herself with an effort and turned to the boy. 'Well now,' she said, 'let's go and see if we can rescue the ball, shall we? It's just the day for paddling in the pond.'

The boy's quivering lips firmed, and he offered her a halfhearted smile. 'Why did he throw our ball into the pond?' he asked, regaining his confidence, and with it a sense of indignation. 'It won't bounce any more. It'll be all wet and soggy.'

'Let's see, shall we?' Abby accompanied him across the grass, aware of being the cynosure of all eyes. Now she noticed a group of women gathered together at the gate of a cottage on the other side of the green, and two old men, seated on a bench beneath the trees. No doubt they had all seen what happened, she reflected, permitting another glance at Matthew's retreating back. Perhaps she should have made him rescue the ball as he was the one who had thrown it, but at the time she had been too incensed with his behaviour to think of that.

The ducks were gradually returning to the pond, and the children trailed after Abby and her companion, whispering and giggling among themselves. One or two of them addressed her ginger-headed escort, but most of them were content to wait and see what was going to happen.

The ball had come to the surface, and was bobbing about in the water just out of reach. Abby found a piece

53

of twig and jabbed at it ineffectually, but every time she got near it the ball just bobbed away.

'D'you want me to get it?' A little girl with long brown plaits, and wearing a tee-shirt and shorts, was already kicking off her sandals, but Abby hastily demurred. She had no idea how deep the water might be in the middle of the pond, and the last thing she needed right now was some irate mother charging her with putting her daughter's life in jeopardy.

'I'll get it,' she averred, mentally cringing at the idea of putting her feet into the pond's murky waters. She bent and unbuckled her sandals and rolled up the hems of her jeans. 'Step back, all of you. I don't want you to get splashed.'

The pond water was just as unpleasant to step into as she had expected. Her feet made a horrible squelching sound as they encountered the silt at the bottom of the pond, and she dreaded to think what unspeakable filth she might be standing in.

'Can I be of some assistance?'

'Daddy!'

The two exclamations were made almost simultaneously, and the little girl who had offered to help Abby turned to greet a stocky, broad-shouldered man, casually attired in cotton trousers and an open-necked shirt. His shirt sleeves were rolled back to his elbows, and there was a smudge of red paint on the knee of his cream slacks. But his expression was amused and friendly, and Abby was grateful to see an uncensorious face.

'I think I can manage,' she replied rather ruefully, grimacing as she captured the elusive ball. 'There we are— I've got it. But thanks for the offer anyway.'

'My pleasure.' The man leant forward to offer her his hand as she stepped out on to the grass. 'I guess I came too late, but I was painting, and I had to wash my hands.' He nodded at her dirty feet. 'It was good of you to help them. They've all been told to keep out of the pond.'

'It wasn't our fault.'

A chorus of indignant voices strove to put their point of

view, but the man held up his hand to silence them.

'I'm Sean Willis,' he said, ignoring the children's chatter. 'And you must be Miss Caldwell's niece. I recognised you from the photograph she has beside her bed.'

'Sean Willis!' Abby made a not very successful effort to dry her feet on the grass. 'Then you're——'

'—your aunt's doctor,' he inserted cheerfully, as the youngsters began to drift away. 'She told me you were coming. I'm very grateful to you.'

'Oh——' Abby made a deprecating gesture, 'it was the least I could do.'

'Well, I hope you've had some success with Miss Caldwell. It really is imperative that we make her see reason.'

Abby looked down at her feet, wondering why she didn't simply tell him that she planned to stay. She was sure he would approve, but she wasn't sure of the wisdom of them staying any more. Not after this afternoon. Not after Matthew had behaved so badly. How could they stay here if things were going to get worse, instead of better? It wouldn't be fair to Aunt Hannah, let alone anyone else.

'Oh, I say——' Sean Willis misinterpreted her silence, and gestured towards her feet, 'you can't go home like that. You'll ruin your sandals if you attempt to put them on. Look, my house is just across the green. Why don't you allow me to offer you washing facilities, at least? Miranda can come with us, just so those old women don't get the wrong impression.'

Abby looked up. 'But won't your wife——'

'My wife's dead, Mrs Roth. Unfortunately, she contracted leukaemia when Miranda was only a few months old. I have a housekeeper, a Mrs Davison, who is a treasure, but she's away today, shopping in Newcastle, and I've been trying a bit of do-it-yourself, not very successfully, I'm afraid.'

Abby gave in to his persuasion. Apart from anything else, she would welcome a cooling-off period before she followed Matthew back to the cottage, and in any case, he was right; she couldn't possibly put on her sandals before she had washed her feet.

The only obstacle came when they reached the road that circled the green, and divided the stretch of smooth grass from the path to his front door. 'You'll have to carry her, Daddy,' Miranda directed, as Abby put her foot gingerly on to the gravel.

'Why didn't I think of that?' declared Sean gaily, swinging Abby off her feet, before she had chance to protest. 'Let's really give the gossips something to chew over. Would you like me to carry you over the threshold?'

'That won't be necessary.' Abby insisted he put her down on the concrete path. 'If you'd like to fetch a dish of water out here. I can sit on your steps in full view of everyone.'

'I wouldn't hear of it.' Sean shook his head severely. 'And from what I hear from your aunt, you're not afraid of a bit of gossip yourself. Mind the paintwork in the hall. That's what I was doing, when I saw you going for a swim.'

The house Abby entered was square and old, twin leaded windows flanking a studded front door. Beyond the door, a narrow hall ran from front to back, and because Sean was painting, there were newspapers instead of carpets on the floor.

'Come into the cloakroom,' he said, as his daughter laid Abby's sandals at the foot of the stairs. 'Miranda, go and get a dish out of the kitchen. And fetch one of the towels Mrs Davison had hanging on the dryer.'

'I'm very grateful,' Abby said a few minutes later, emerging from the cloakroom feeling clean again. 'That water really was foul. I'm surprised the ducks aren't poisoned.'

'Oh, you'd be surprised what ducks can stand,' remarked Sean cheerfully, inviting her into the room across the hall. 'Come along. I've made some tea. You've given me an ideal excuse to take a break, and I'm not going to let you go without humouring me.'

Abby's hesitation was barely perceptible, and she

preceded him into a comfortable sitting room to find that they were alone.

'I've let Miranda go back to play,' he declared, ushering her on to the couch and taking his place beside her. 'Now, will you be mother or shall I? I take both milk and two sugars, if you should decide to take charge.'

Abby smiled, and immediately tackled the cups on the low table set in front of her. There was cream and sugar, and a plate of rich tea biscuits, as well as a fat-bellied teapot. She poured the tea carefully, making sure she didn't spill any on the table's polished surface, and then settled back with her own, relaxing almost without realising it.

'How long are you staying, Mrs Roth?' Sean asked, helping himself to biscuits and dunking them in his tea. 'I'm sure Miss Caldwell was delighted to see you. She tells me you haven't visited Rothside once since you left.'

Put like that, it sounded awful, and Abby strove to explain: 'It's a long journey,' she ventured rather lamely. 'But Aunt Hannah has been to visit me. Not once, but several times.'

'Yes, so she said.' Sean frowned. 'I suppose it is an expensive trip. Rail fares can be prohibitive.'

'Yes.' Abby let it go at that, and presently her companion changed the subject.

'You're lucky it's such a fine weekend. Rothside can be grim when the weather's bad. But I suppose you know that, coming from these parts. I'm afraid I was born and brought up in Hampshire, where we don't get such extremes.'

Abby nodded. 'Have you been in Rothside long, Dr Willis?'

'Sean, please,' he averred, taking another biscuit. 'And yes, I've lived here—let me see, it must be almost ten years now. I suppose you knew Dr Morrison. He probably retired soon after you moved away.'

'Yes.'

Once again Abby was left without any means of prolonging the conversation, and deciding he was owed an explanation about the afternoon's events, she told him about Matthew.

'I don't know what got into him,' she murmured, finishing her tea and putting down her cup. 'He generally gets on with children. I suppose I should have made him retrieve the ball, but I was so angry, I just sent him home.'

Sean nodded. 'I saw him. He's a big boy for what— twelve? Thirteen?'

'He's almost twelve,' Abby replied tautly. 'I'm afraid his size is against him. People invariably expect more of him because they think he's older.'

'You must have been very young when you had him, Mrs Roth.'

'I—I was eighteen,' said Abby, getting to her feet. 'I really mustn't hold you up any longer, Dr Willis. The tea was delicious, but I really should be going.'

'All right.' Sean rose too, and Abby realised that in her high-heeled sandals, they were more or less on eye level. Yet for all that, he gave the impression of being bigger, probably because of his bulk. She wondered how old he was. Between thirty-five and forty, she imagined. Piers' age actually, although there was no other resemblance between the two men. Sean was more like Tristan Oliver had been, sturdier and more stolid. The kind of man one could depend on, she thought, moving towards the door. Honest and trustworthy, and totally reliable.

'Will I see you before you leave?' he asked, as Abby started down the path. 'I believe Miss Caldwell said you were staying for the weekend. Will you still be here on Monday morning?'

'I'm afraid not.' Whatever she decided, Abby knew she would have to return to London, if only to sort out her affairs. 'But perhaps we'll meet again before long. Thank you for the tea, it was just what I needed.'

'Any time.' Sean accompanied her down the path. 'Come back soon.'

Abby found her cheeks were quite warm as she walked away across the green. She was aware of Sean watching her, and paused once to glance back and wave. But the undivided attention of onlookers deterred her from repeating her action, and she quickened her step as Ivy Cottage came in sight.

Abby broke her change of heart to Hannah the following morning. She had not felt able to tell the old lady the night before, what with Matthew sulking in his room upstairs and her own nerves shredded by his insolent behaviour. But on Sunday morning she knew she could delay no longer, and as they scraped the potatoes for lunch, she admitted that she had had second thoughts about moving.

'But, Abby——' Hannah gazed at her niece with eyes suddenly filled with tears, 'you promised! You said you'd give it a try, and you can't go back on your word now. If you don't stay, Dr Willis will make me go into Rosemount, and I won't last six weeks if I have to leave the cottage.'

Abby sighed. 'Aunt Hannah, Dr Willis is not the monster you're making him out to be. I've met him, remember?' She had given her aunt an edited version of all that had happened the previous afternoon. 'He's only concerned with what's best for you.' If you insist on staying here, then other arrangements will have to be made.'

'I know—a companion, like you said,' exclaimed Hannah, dabbing her eyes with the corner of her apron. 'Oh, Abby, why have you changed your mind? Aren't you happy here? Is it something I've done? If you'd just tell me——'

'It's nothing like that.' Abby felt mean. 'Please don't look so woebegone. I'm not saying I won't come and visit you. Now that I've been here, I'll come again. But I really think it might be better for Matthew if he isn't uprooted from his familiar environment. He wouldn't fit in here, Aunt Hannah. It's asking too much.'

It was hard leaving, particularly as Matthew had barely addressed two words to her since the previous afternoon. Abby felt near to tears herself when Aunt Hannah hugged them both goodbye, and as the taxi sped towards Alnbury, where they were to catch the bus to Newcastle, she was glad of Matthew's silence to recover her composure.

During the tense week that followed, no mention was made of Abby's reasons for abandoning her intention to move to Rothside. Matthew went off to school as usual, and she had her work, although gradually that was running down, and she guessed Trevor was only keeping her on out of kindness. Nevertheless, she tried to maintain the façade that everything was as it should be until ten days later, when her small world exploded.

It had been a day much like any other, and Abby was about to leave the office early, at about half past three, when a policeman appeared in the glass-walled reception area beyond her office. Susie, the office junior, who generally attended to visitors, had already left, and Abby emerged from her office enquiringly, wondering what Trevor could have done.

'Mrs Roth?'

The fact that the policeman knew her name was disturbing, but Abby refused to panic. Trevor could have been in touch with the police, he could have asked them to contact her, as his secretary. There was no earthly need for her to jump to hasty and probably erroneous conclusions.

'Yes,' she answered now, unable to prevent her hand from straying nervously to her hair. 'Can I help you?'

'I hope so.' The policeman was young and diffident, but evidently intent on doing his duty. 'It's about your son, Mrs Roth: we've got him down at the station. He and two other boys were picked up in Marburys this afternoon. They'd been shoplifting.'

Abby's legs gave out on her, and she sought Susie's chair weakly, gazing up at the young policeman with wide disbelieving eyes. 'But I thought he was at school——' she blurted helplessly, and the policeman nodded, as if expecting this answer.

'According to his form-master, Matthew has been playing truant for some time. I believe he spoke to you about it a couple of weeks ago.'

'Well, yes. Yes, he did.' Abby tried to think coherently. 'I went to see him—just after the new term started. He told me that—that Matt would have to pay more attention to his lessons, but I never dreamt——' She broke off abruptly, and then stumbled on: 'You see—he shouldn't have been at that school last term, but the infant and junior school he'd been attending had closed down, and rather than send the children to an entirely different school, just for one term, they took them into the comprehensive at Easter.' She paused. 'He's an impressionable boy, constable, and he got in with the wrong group from the start——'

The constable made an understanding gesture, evidently moved by Abby's impassioned outburst. But he had his job to do, and tucking the helmet he had removed under his arm, he said: 'I suggest you come down to the station with me now, and explain the situation to Sergeant Hodges, Mrs Roth. I'm sure he'll be sympathetic, he has children of his own.'

Trevor offered to go with her, but Abby declined. 'I think it's more appropriate if I go alone,' she said, realising how easily situations could be misconstrued. Her position was not ideal as it was, she and Matthew living apart from his father, with no other means of support than her job, which was soon to be axed. They asked such awkward questions, she remembered that from when Matthew was a baby, and she was first starting out on her own. What if they thought she wasn't a fit mother? What if they tried to take Matthew away from her? Surely first offenders were not sent to approved school or Borstal, or any of those disciplinary establishments.

Matthew and the two other boys were waiting in an anteroom at the police station, overseen by another policeman and a policewoman. Abby was relieved to see that her son looked suitably apprehensive, although his expression grew sullen when he saw her.

The interview with Sergeant Hodges in his office was not pleasant. Marburys was one of the biggest supermarket chains in the country, and it appeared that this was not the first time the boys had been observed acting suspiciously. Apparently, on those other occasions, nothing could be proved, but this afternoon the boys had been observed entering the store, and the necessary action had been taken.

Abby didn't know what to say. Her feeble explanations about Matthew being too young, about him falling into bad company, did not move the hardbitten sergeant, and it was his information, he said, that far from being led by his companions, Matthew had been the leader. He would be expected to appear at the juvenile court the next morning, and pending the magistrates' decision, the case would probably be postponed until preliminary reports had been prepared.

'Juvenile courts are more concerned with protecting the child's interests than meting out punishment,' Sergeant Hodges declared quietly, speaking privately to Abby before she left. 'It will depend a lot on the report given by his headmaster.' He shrugged. 'If this is just a flash in the pan, he'll probably get off with just a warning. This time.'

'Thank you, sergeant.' Abby was grateful for this small piece of reassurance, but her heart sank at the prospect of dealing with Matthew, after this latest upheaval.

They walked back to the flat, Matthew with his hands sunk deep into the pockets of his trousers, his mouth compressed stubbornly as Abby attempted to reason with him.

'You realise you've jeopardised your future, don't you?' she exclaimed, shaking her head. 'Mr Braintree will probably expel you from Southfield, and if they send you to another school, you'll already be labelled a troublemaker before you start.'

'So what? Brainless can do what he likes. I don't care.'

'Well, I do.'

'You go to school, then,' retorted Matthew sullenly. 'I don't need education. Only fools and idiots believe it makes a scrap of difference to someone like me.'

'Someone like you!' Abby stared at him. 'What do you mean?'

Matthew shrugged. 'I'm going to make a lot of money. I'm going to buy a big house and ride around in a big car.'

'And how do you propose to earn that kind of money if you don't have any qualifications?' Abby asked wearily.

'Who says I'm going to earn it?' demanded Matthew scornfully. 'There are other ways . . .'

Abby's head was throbbing. 'Matt, stop talking like this! I've got a headache, and you're not making it any better. Don't you have any conscience at all? You took sweets and cigarettes without paying for them. You stayed away from school, when you knew I believed you were there. Don't you care about me? Have I suddenly ceased to mean anything to you?'

Matthew didn't answer, and Abby knew an over-whelming sense of defeat. If she couldn't appeal to his better nature, was there any hope for them at all? Somehow she had the feeling that the barrier between them was rapidly climbing out of reach.

There was no point in returning to work that day. Sending Matthew up to the flat, Abby rang Trevor from the public callbox downstairs giving him a brief outline of what had happened.

'I'll have to go to court with him in the morning,' she added. 'Is that all right?'

'Take the day off,' declared Trevor magnanimously. 'Goodness knows, there's nothing spoiling. As a matter of fact, Abby, if you find anything else to do just let me know. I'd be happy to pay your salary in lieu of notice. In fact, if you'd like to take the remainder of the week off, feel free. I'll let you know if there's any change in the circumstances.'

Going up in the lift, Abby reflected that this was Trevor's polite way of telling her he had nothing for her to do. It was frightening to think that in two weeks she was going to be out of work. The image of the unemployment office loomed large ahead of her, and the spectre of all the personal details she was going to have to reveal to some anonymous bureaucrat filled her with despair.

She heard voices as she entered the flat, but she didn't pay them any attention. She assumed Matthew had switched on the television set, as usual, and she was so absorbed with her own miseries, she had hung up her jacket and opened the living room door before realising anyone else was present.

'You can turn that off——' she was beginning tersely, as she entered the room, only to break off abruptly at the sight of the tall dark man standing by the window. Matthew was propped against the sideboard, his shoulders hunched aggressively, his fair features flushed and resentful. Unlike the first occasion when he had met his father, he was silent and evidently subdued, and Abby gazed at him bewilderedly before turning her attention to Piers.

Piers seemed quite at his ease, only the faint tightness about his mouth revealing any hint of his emotions. In a three-piece navy lounge suit, the jacket of which was looped carelessly over one shoulder, as if he found the day too warm, he looked calm and unruffled, and Abby envied him his ability to fight free of responsibility.

Then, like a bolt from the blue, the solution for him being there struck her. It had to be Aunt Hannah, she thought with dismay. She must have had a second attack; perhaps she was gravely ill or worse! With a moan of anguish, she pressed her trembling hands to her lips, feeling without being able to stop them the sting of the tears that could no longer be denied.

'For God's sake, Abby, it's not as bad as all that!'

Piers' harsh tones revived Abby's flagging spirit. With a determined effort she scrubbed her palms across her damp cheeks, and faced him bravely. The last thing she needed right now was for him to feel sorry for her. Whatever had happened, she would face it as she faced everything else, and she forced herself to wonder what he had said to Matthew to explain her son's red-faced indignation.

'What did the police say?' Piers demanded, before Abby

could make any response, and she gazed at him blankly. 'I expect they told you he'll probably get off with a caution. That may be of some consolation to you, I suppose, although I'm of the opinion that a more traditional form of punishment produces better results.'

'It's nothing to do with you,' muttered Matthew, as Abby realised what Piers was talking about. She was surprised Matthew had told him. It was not something she would have expected him to brag about.

'When I came to the flat and you weren't here, I went to your place of work,' Piers was explaining now, ignoring the boy's outburst. 'I spoke to a man called—Bourne?'

'Trevor?' Abby was surprised. 'But I've just spoken to him on the phone. He didn't say anything to me.'

'I didn't give my name,' said Piers flatly. 'Perhaps he thought I was some sort of official. At any rate, he told me where you were, and what had happened.'

Thank you, Trevor, thought Abby wearily, and then: 'But why are you here? Is—is it Aunt Hannah? Is she worse? Couldn't Dr Willis have phoned me if—if there was some change in her condition?'

Piers' lips twisted. 'You know Sean Willis, I believe.'

'I have met him, yes.' Abby was growing impatient now. 'Piers, if there's something wrong with Aunt Hannah——'

'So far as I'm aware, your aunt is not in any immediate danger——'

'*Danger!*'

'Abby, she's not ill—at least, no more so than she was when you came up to Rothside. The situation hasn't changed. That's not why I'm here.'

'Then why——'

Piers cast a pointed look in Matthew's direction. 'Could we speak privately, Abby? I have something I want to discuss with you. Something your aunt did ask me to talk to you about.'

'Aunt Hannah?' Abby was uneasy. 'If it's about the divorce, then I think Matt——'

'It's not about the divorce,' said Piers heavily. 'Now, if you don't mind——'

Abby hesitated, then she shook her head. 'Go to your room, Matt,' she requested quietly. 'I'll come and speak to you in a few minutes.'

'I don't see why——' began Matthew sulkily, only to have his father intervene.

'Your room, Matthew,' he said, brooking no argument, and the boy responded to his tone with sullen, but instinctive, obedience.

When the door to Matthew's bedroom had closed, Abby drew an unsteady breath. 'Well?' she said, twisting her hands together. 'What did Aunt Hannah say to you? I can't believe, whatever it was, it caused you to come all this way to see us.'

'You're right.' Piers swung his jacket off his shoulder and dropped it on to the sofa. 'My reasons for being in London have nothing to do with you.'

'I thought not.' Abby held up her head. 'Did Aunt Hannah ask you to come and see me? I suppose she told you what she wanted me to do? Well, don't worry, I shan't be returning to Rothside. I have quite enough problems to cope with as it is.'

'So I see.' Piers hooked his thumbs in the back of his belt. 'Since when has Matthew been in trouble with the police?'

'Since today.' Abby's nails dug into her palms. 'Piers, say what you have to say, will you? I really don't have the patience for small talk today.'

'Small talk,' he echoed flatly. 'Is that what you call it?'

'Yes—no—oh, I don't know.' Abby put up an unsteady hand to her temple. 'Piers, I don't know why you've come here, but I can do without your opinion of Matt's behaviour. All right, so I know he's becoming a problem. But he's my problem, not yours, as you pointed out the other day.'

Piers' eyes darkened. 'You never give up, do you, Abby? Any chance to turn the screw.'

'To turn the screw!' Abby caught her breath. 'How do you think I feel every time you deny he's your son?'

Piers bent his head. 'That's something else.'

'Is it?' Abby was angry. 'As far as I can see it's all the same thing. You abandoned your responsibilities more than eleven years ago. You have no right now to question my methods of bringing him up.'

'All right.' Piers controlled any urge he might have had to retaliate in kind and spread his hands. 'I didn't come here to get into an argument about Matthew. I called to see your aunt yesterday. As you suggested, she did tell me what she'd asked you to do.'

'Did she?' Abby turned away. 'Why should she do that? What did you say to her?'

'Nothing you couldn't have overheard,' Piers retorted mildly. 'Abby, why didn't you tell me about this when we spoke together? Instead of using me as an excuse for you to remain in London!'

'Using you?'

'Well, didn't you? Didn't you tell Miss Caldwell that I would object to your returning to Rothside?'

'And wouldn't you?' Abby countered, turning back on him.

Piers hesitated. 'I can't stop you from living wherever you choose.'

'And Matthew?'

'What about Matthew?'

'Am I expected to hide his identity?'

Piers sighed. 'Matthew's identity, as you call it, is a matter for your own conscience.'

'You—prig!'

Piers took a deep breath. 'I think this has gone far enough, Abby. So far as I'm concerned you can tell people what the hell you like! When the divorce is through, I shall be marrying Val Langton, and it won't matter a damn what lies you tell about me.'

'Lies!' Abby gazed at him frustratedly for a second, and then turned away. 'Get out of here!' she commanded, her voice breaking on a sob. 'For God's sake, get out of here, before I throw up!'

'Abby . . .' Piers stepped closer to her, his nearness

devastating her crumbling defences. 'Why do you do this, Abby? Why do you deliberately provoke me? Does it give you a masochistic kind of satisfaction? Is that how you get your kicks these days, by inflicting pain on yourself and everyone around you?'

'No!' Abby moved abruptly away from him. 'Please go, Piers. We have nothing more to say to one another.'

'And what are you going to do?'

'What's that to you?'

'I want to know, Abby.'

'What do you think?' Schooling her features, she forced herself to turn and face him again. 'Go on with my life as before. What else can I do?'

'You can come back to Rothside, as your aunt wants you to do. She told me about your job. And the boy will have the chance to make a new start.'

'The boy, as you call him, resents everything I do for him.' Abby fumbled for her handkerchief. 'And—and your coming here isn't helping matters. Can't you see, you're only encouraging him to—to believe——'

'—that I'm his father,' Piers finished heavily. 'All right, you have a point there. But coming back to Rothside, that's something else. At least, no one can deny that that's where he belongs. And I'm sure the Olivers——'

'*Get out!*' Abby practically screamed the words at him, and as if realising she was near to breaking point, Piers moved towards the door.

'Think about what I said,' he advised, draping his jacket over his shoulder again, but his suggestion elicited no response from Abby's shaking frame.

CHAPTER FIVE

ABBY came out of court the next morning feeling numb. She couldn't believe what had taken place, and even Matthew looked somewhat dazed by what had happened. For some reason best known to himself, Piers had made himself responsible for Matthew's good behaviour. He had sent his own solicitor, Miles Shand, to attend the hearing, and overriding any objections Abby might have cared to make, the lawyer had politely stated that Mrs Roth would be returning to the north of England, to facilitate her husband's action on the boy's behalf.

Abby had been totally bemused. While the practical side of her brain was telling her that Piers had no right to exert his authority over them, when at no time in the past had he acknowledged the boy's existence, her emotions were aroused by Matthew's undisguised excitement. Far from resenting his father's intervention, he reacted on instinct, no doubt imagining Piers was prepared to assume a full role in his life from now on. How could she disillusion him? Abby wondered. How could she explain that all Piers had done was use his own considerable influence as a magistrate to sway the London magistrate's verdict, and in so doing forcing them to return to Rothside?

'A satisfactory conclusion, Mrs Roth.' Miles Shand was suddenly beside her, smiling at Matthew and shaking her hand. 'Now, all that's necessary is for you to make the necessary arrangements about your removal. Mr Roth has no doubt explained that you can leave all that safely in our hands.'

'No.' Abby's voice was curt, but she couldn't help it. 'No, Mr Shand, Mr Roth didn't tell us anything. But I'd very much like to speak with him if that could be arranged.'

'Arranged?' Miles Shand looked taken aback. 'But

surely you know: Mr Roth was obliged to return to Rothside this morning. The—er—the person he was travelling with had to get back, and as he was driving this person——'

'I presume you mean Miss Langton,' Abby said tersely, and Miles Shand looked relieved.

'Ah, yes, of course. Of course, Mrs Roth, you would know about that. Well, as I say, they had to get back, so I'm afraid you'll have to wait until you get to Rothside to speak to your husband.'

'You know, I suppose, that Piers has applied for a divorce.'

The lawyer looked a little discomfited now. 'Is that so?'

'Surely you knew.'

'Well, Mr Roth may have said something——'

'I'm sure he did.'

'But this doesn't fundamentally alter the circumstances of the case, Mrs Roth. I mean, divorce is for the parents, not the children.'

'Mum!'

Matthew was beginning to look uncomfortable now, and realising if she said much more she would destroy his hopes completely, Abby shook her head. She had no idea what was in Piers' mind, and until she had spoken to him, she couldn't make snap judgements. But one thing was certain, once again the Roths had taken a hand in her affairs, and once again she and Matthew were the victims.

The journey back to Northumberland was almost a fac-simile of the first. As the express sped northwards, Abby reflected how ironic it was that this time they should be returning at Piers' instigation. Only a month ago he had declared he never wanted to see her again, and now here they were, hurtling back at his invitation.

But why? What motive did he have for changing his mind so abruptly? She couldn't believe he had suddenly conceived a conscience about his son. He hardly knew the boy, and what he did know was not appealing. There had to be another reason, and she racked her brains to find it as the train covered the miles between London and Newcastle.

Matthew himself had been amazingly docile since the court hearing. Abby told herself it was because he hadn't returned to school, and therefore had avoided contact with the boys she was sure had influenced his behaviour, but she wasn't convinced. The disturbing truth was that Matthew was expecting more of his father than Piers even imagined, and Abby dreaded to think what might happen when her son discovered he had been deceived.

The arrangements for moving had been completed without difficulties. Piers' solicitors had arranged the storage of Abby's furniture—she had refused to sell on the grounds that if she and Matthew ever got a home of their own she would need it—and Trevor Bourne had been extremely generous, and insisted on giving Abby a little nest-egg: 'Just in case you ever need it.'

The money had already come in useful. With Matthew's consent—if not with his actual encouragement—Abby had bought him a pair of decent boots—not the sensible walking shoes she would have preferred, but at least the kind of footwear that did not look out of place with his school uniform. His hair, too, had grown in the weeks since he first came to Rothside, and although it was still short, it lay more smoothly against his head. It made him look older, more mature, and Abby knew a fleeting pang for the baby he had once been. She would have liked to have had more children, if things had been different. Despite the difficulties, her pregnancy and Matthew's subsequent birth had been relatively easy, and the doctor at the hospital in London had said that she was a natural mother. At the time, she had not wanted to hear it, with the pain of Piers' accusations still ringing in her ears. But now, from the distance of almost twelve years, she could view it more objectively, and she knew that those weeks and months when Matthew was developing from a helpless suckling to a loving, affectionate individual had possessed a satisfaction not even Piers could take away.

The train arrived in Newcastle at six o'clock. It was a chilly October evening; the nights were drawing in, and it would be dark long before they got to Alnbury. Abby would have caught the earlier train, but Miles Shand had booked their seats and bought their tickets, and she could hardly go and change them, when he had gone to so much trouble. It was the first time she had travelled first class on a train, and although she had been tempted to sit in the second class carriages, she could not deny Matthew his brief taste of indulgence. The train had not been full, and he had spent the journey shifting from one side of the carriage to the other, sometimes sharing her table, with its two empty seats, and at others sitting at one of the tables for two, stretching his legs expansively.

They had more luggage this time, Abby choosing to fetch most of their clothes with them, the remainder following with her more personal possessions. It meant Matthew had two suitcases to hoist along the platform, and Abby carried the holdall, along with her vanity case and handbag.

'Let me take that. I've got a porter waiting at the barrier,' Piers stated abruptly, appearing out of the crowd. He took one of Matthew's suitcases, and the holdall from Abby's unresisting fingers, before striding away along the platform, his lean frame dealing flexibly with the other travellers.

'Hey, he's come to meet us this time,' Matthew declared, grinning at his mother. 'Come on, Mum, don't dawdle! He's probably parked where he was before, and you know he almost got a ticket.'

Abby followed her son with some reluctance. What was Piers trying to do? She should have expected something of the kind when Miles Shand insisted on arranging their tickets, but somehow that had seemed part and parcel with her moving, and nothing to do with Piers at all. Now she saw how wrong she had been. Miles Shand had just been acting under orders. But what was Piers hoping to achieve, and didn't Valerie Langton object to his sudden concern for a child he had hitherto ignored?

At the other side of the barrier, Piers relieved Matthew of the second case, and dumping it on the porter's trolley along with the others, he instructed the man to follow them outside. 'The car's parked in a no-waiting area,' he remarked dryly, 'but it's worth the fine not to have to park half a mile away.'

Matthew exchanged a knowing look with his mother, as if to say 'I told you so' and then walked confidently away beside his father. With a distinctly hollow feeling inside, Abby was obliged to follow them.

Their cases were stowed in the boot of the Daimler, and Piers indicated that Matthew should get in the back. 'Your mother can sit in front,' he said, arousing the first scowl of disappointment from his son. 'Get in, Matthew. You're holding us up. Abby—here you are. Give me your make-up case. I'll take care of that.'

'Mum, couldn't I sit in front?' Matthew pleaded, making no move to obey his father. 'I've never sat in the front seat of a car before. I bet you have loads of times.'

'In the back, Matthew.' Piers' tone was sharpened by impatience. 'Abby, get inside, will you? Do you want me arrested?'

Abby sighed. 'Matthew could sit——'

'Inside!' Piers hesitated no longer, swinging open the rear door and thrusting the boy into the back. Then he looked at Abby, and glimpsing the steely determination in his eyes, she got into the front without another word, aware as she did so that any recalcitrance on her part could only react badly on Matthew.

The city was busy with early evening traffic, and for a time Piers was too intent on negotiating the traffic to pay any attention to his passengers. But eventually they emerged on to the Jedburgh road, and he was able to relax and ask them about their journey.

Abby had had two weeks to get over his arbitrary use of his authority, two weeks to come to terms with his decision to play a part, albeit a small one, in Matthew's future. In the beginning, she had been full of resentment, furious that he should have acted so high-handedly, and without consulting her. When she had first recovered from the shock, she had wanted to reconvene the hearing, to argue with the magistrate, to explain that Piers had no real intention of getting involved with his son.

But she hadn't. Common sense, and the well-meant if pedantic advice of Miles Shand had persuaded her that by acting on impulse she stood to lose everything. She was in rather a dubious position, he said. While Matthew was, and had been, actually in her charge since his birth, he was still nominally Piers' son. The fact that he was a persistent truant and was now in trouble with the law was bound to count against her. As, too, were her own uncertain circumstances.

Piers, conversely, had many points in his favour. He was well off, for one thing; his character was impeccable, and his position as a magistrate more than qualified him as a suitable person to have custody of a minor. Abby reserved her own opinion as to Piers' character, but she could quite see that while he might not want custody of Matthew, she dared not run the risk of some social worker recommending he be taken into care by the local authorities.

Now, however, when Piers spoke to her, she knew an almost overwhelming urge to demand how he had had the nerve to overrule her authority as he had. How dared he behave as if his meeting them at the station was the most natural thing in the world? she seethed. Didn't he see what he was doing? Didn't he care what effect his behaviour would have on Matthew? He had said he didn't want the boy to get hurt, yet it seemed he was doing everything in his power to cripple him emotionally. It was cruel!

As if sensing the animosity Abby was endeavouring to control, Piers glanced her way, and although Abby knew he couldn't see her expression, she deliberately turned her head. She didn't want to talk to him. She didn't even want to look at him, and she stiffened with resentment when Matthew answered his father's questions instead.

Apparently Matthew had got over his disappointment at having to ride in the back, and listening to them talking together, Abby knew a helpless sense of outrage. Why was it that when she scolded Matthew for any misdemeanour, he always took umbrage and sulked for hours, yet on the two occasions Piers had admonished him, he had scarcely taken offence?

'Is something wrong?' Piers eventually asked the question in an undertone, when Matthew, having exhausted the topic of high-speed trains and any subsequent competition they might give to the airlines, was idly watching the retreating lights of other cars out of the rear window. 'You haven't said a word since I met you. Why do I get the feeling that you'd rather have caught the bus?'

'Because I would,' declared Abby childishly, refusing to respond to his humour. 'What are you trying to do, Piers? Destroy what little chance of communication Matt and I have left?'

The way his fingers tightened on the wheel spoke of his irritation, but Piers' tone was still mild as he responded. 'I thought this was what you wanted, Abby,' he declared, without taking his eyes from the road. 'I'm acknowledging Matthew as an individual. I'm prepared to accept that as he bears my name, I have some responsibility for him. Whatever my personal feelings are, I'm willing to help you now, if I can, if only because you seem to need help badly.'

Abby's angrily indrawn breath caused him to lift a warning hand. 'Later,' he said flatly, casting a significant glance over his shoulder. 'We'll talk about it later. Right now, tell me whether Shand lived up to my expectations. He's a pompous little man, but he means well.'

Abby's teeth jarred together. 'Mr Shand did as you told him,' she declared shortly. 'He forced me to accept the magistrate's verdict, as you knew he would. Tell me, does Miss Langton approve of your actions on our behalf?'

Piers gave her a wry look. 'Val knows what I'm doing,' he replied levelly. 'But she doesn't own me. I've chosen to make Matt my concern, and she accepts it. In fact, she's looking forward to meeting him again. Does that answer your question?'

Abby gasped. 'She's looking forward to meeting him again!' she echoed.

'That's what I said.' Piers lifted his shoulders carelessly. 'Abby, surely you realised that I couldn't adopt Matthew nominally without enforcing it in fact?'

Abby's lips parted. 'Adopt!'

'Not literally.' Piers spoke in a low impatient tone. 'Abby, when I agreed to take responsibility for Matthew, I knew what I was doing. I knew what it would mean.' He sighed. 'Look, I know this may be hard for you to accept, but I am acting in the boy's best interests. My involvement has to be seen to be working. The social worker assigned to Matthew's case will expect me to be involved. There's still a report to be filed, and his future behaviour to be ensured.'

'I know that.' But Abby had not known that Piers was going to take his job so seriously. With this, as with everything else, she had completely misinterpreted his intentions, and she needed time to absorb this and consider what it might mean.

'Are we nearly there?'

Matthew had grown tired of watching the other vehicles and now came to drape his arms over the front seats. Had he heard what they had been saying? Abby wondered apprehensively. Had he understood it if he had? And what did Piers really mean to do for the boy? She had the uneasy feeling he intended to make her regret taunting him about his responsibilities.

'Another fifteen minutes,' Piers answered now, when Abby made no response, and Matthew sighed. 'Why? Are you hungry? I suppose in the normal way you'd have had your evening meal by now.'

'I'm okay.' Matthew watched the dials and switches glowing on the dashboard. 'How fast can this car go, really flat out, I mean?'

Piers glanced Abby's way. 'Quite fast,' he said, making

no boast about the car's top speed. 'But the speed limit on English roads is seventy miles an hour, so it isn't very sensible to drive beyond the limit.'

'But you have.' Matthew was not to be put off.

'Occasionally,' agreed Piers dryly.

'I knew it.' Matthew looked pleased with himself. 'When I grow up, I'm going to buy a Mercedes.'

'Are you?' Once again, Piers exchanged a look with Abby. 'Well, I suggest you've got a long way to go before that happens. So I shouldn't build my hopes up too soon.'

'Only five years,' declared Matthew indignantly. 'They'll soon pass. When I'm seventeen——'

'When you're seventeen, you'll still be at school,' inserted Piers flatly, and Matthew caught his breath.

'No, I won't. I'm leaving school at sixteen, didn't Mum tell you? Exams, qualifications, they're not for me. I want to be free, I want to travel——'

'You can't do much travelling without any money,' retorted Piers flatly.

'I'll get money.'

'How?'

Matthew was silent.

'By robbing another supermarket?' enquired Piers caustically. 'Or did you have something more lucrative in mind?'

Matthew grunted, 'Mum did tell you, didn't she?'

'Your mother's told me nothing about your plans for your future. But I'll tell you mine, shall I?'

'If you like.' Matthew shrugged indifferently, but Abby listened intently as Piers outlined his proposals.

'You'll stay at school until you're eighteen,' he said dispassionately. 'And, if you've got the brains, you'll go on to university.'

'University!' Matthew sounded disgusted.

'Yes, university,' Piers repeated, unmoved. 'Don't knock it until you try it. I'll tell you, it beats the hell out of working for a living!'

Matthew pulled a face. 'It's just another name for school!'

'No, it's not. It's nothing like school,' retorted Piers
with emphasis. 'To begin with it's up to you how much
work you do or don't do. You're independent. You're free
to choose. And, if they throw you out after the first year,
you'll have proved you shouldn't be there in the first
place.'

Matthew showed a reluctant interest. 'Did you go to
university?'

'Yes.'

'Which university did you go to?'

'London.'

'London!'

Matthew was actually sounding a little enthusiastic
now, but Abby thought this conversation had gone far
enough. 'Universities cost money,' she said. 'A lot of
money. And Matthew knows that it's very doubtful
whether I'll be able to afford to send him to university.'

'You won't have to,' said Piers quietly. 'I will.' And
before Abby could make any rejoinder, he turned to
Matthew and pointed out the lights of Rothside just
appearing out of the darkness.

Aunt Hannah was waiting at the door of the cottage
when the Daimler drew to a halt at the garden gate.
'Abby!' she exclaimed warmly, coming to meet them, and
Piers carried the luggage indoors as the old lady greeted
her visitors.

'Come along inside,' she said, as Piers slammed the boot
lid. 'You'll have a cup of tea, won't you, Piers? The
kettle's boiling already.'

'Not tonight,' said Piers, but he softened his refusal with
a wry smile. 'I'll see you tomorrow, Abby,' he added,
walking round the car. 'Goodnight, Matt. Look after your
mother.'

With the door closed behind them, Abby could have
given way to her frustration, but she didn't. Matthew was
regarding her with strangely watchful eyes, and she
guessed he was apprehensive of her reaction to Piers' intentions. So instead she behaved as if their return to
Rothside was the most natural thing in the world, and

not until supper was over, and Matthew was in bed and asleep, did she regale Aunt Hannah with everything that had happened.

'Well, I knew about the court hearing, of course,' said the old lady, pouring Abby a glass of home-made elderberry wine. 'You wrote about it in your letter, and Piers came to see me himself, after he got back from London.' She sighed, handing Abby her glass. 'I hope you'll forgive me for sending Piers to see you like that. I never dreamt it would turn out as it has. I mean—my only intention was to try and persuade you to come back to Rothside. I thought if Piers told you he had no objections you might change your mind.'

Abby shook her head. 'But how did you come to tell him what I'd said? I didn't know you and Piers were so close.'

'Now, Abby,' Hannah seated herself opposite the girl and sipped her wine, 'you know I've known Piers since he was a babe, being pushed round the village by his nursemaid. Oh, I know, I didn't know him well as he grew older, but we are his tenants, Abby, and like his father before him, he does take an interest in our affairs.'

'Doesn't he though?' Abby was bitter, and her aunt gazed at her anxiously.

'Abby, I didn't say anything to Piers about Matthew—it wasn't my place to do so. But he knew what Dr Willis had said, and all I did was tell him I was sorry you couldn't come and solve the problem.'

'Did you tell him I had refused to stay because of him?'

'Not in so many words. But, Abby, it was the case, wasn't it? I mean, it wasn't just Matthew's behaviour that made you change your mind.'

Abby sighed. 'I thought it was.'

'Well, and hasn't it turned out for the best, in the circumstances?' Hannah bent to poke the fire. 'Let's face it, Abby, London is not the most ideal place for a boy like Matthew. There are too many temptations. At least at Rothside he'll have the chance to start again.'

'Will he?' Abby returned her aunt's gaze without conviction. 'I suppose you mean with Piers acknowledging him as a Roth.'

'Yes. He's doing that, isn't he?' Hannah was thoughtful. 'Isn't that what you wanted?'

'Now?' Abby gulped the remainder of her wine and got up from her seat. 'Aunt Hannah, I've brought Matt up single-handed for more than eleven years. Do you think it's fair that Piers should just come along and take that responsibility out of my hands?'

'But I thought Matthew was in trouble, dear. I thought there was some question as to whether you would be allowed to keep him.'

'Who told you that?'

Hannah looked troubled. 'Well, Piers, I think. Abby, you have to admit, Matthew hasn't exactly endeared himself to the authorities. The report from his headmaster was deplorable.'

'Did Piers tell you that as well?'

'He may have done.' Hannah moistened her lips. 'Stop looking so fierce, Abby. Look on the bright side. For more than eleven years, as you say, you've had sole responsibility for the boy. Isn't it about time you had a break? Isn't it time his father took some of the burden off your shoulders?'

Abby's mouth quivered. 'I never regarded Matthew as a burden.'

'Nevertheless, he was. And as he gets older, your job isn't going to get any easier.'

'But Piers still doesn't believe that Matt's his son.' Abby paced the floor frustratedly. 'Aunt Hannah, all he's doing is acknowledging him as bearing the same name.'

'I wonder why.' Hannah gave Abby a speculative look, but her niece's lips only curled.

'Don't think it,' she declared vehemently. 'Piers isn't doing this for me. You know,' she paused, 'I wouldn't put it past him to be doing it for Valerie Langton.'

'For Miss Langton?' Hannah looked puzzled. 'Why?'

'Well, Matt did announce himself to her as Piers' son, didn't he, and Piers didn't deny it. And let's face it, it's a strange father that never sees his child.'

Hannah frowned. 'Even so . . .'

'Even so, I bet that's nearer the truth than anything I've heard so far.' Abby shook her head. 'It makes me sick! Just thinking about the way he made himself Matt's guardian makes me want to throw up. He had no right to do it, no right at all. Poor Matt! I wonder how he'll settle down here. I just hope Piers will leave him alone, once he feels his honour has been satisfied!'

CHAPTER SIX

Surprisingly, Abby slept well, and awakened the next morning feeling more capable of facing whatever was to come. Piers would soon get bored with playing the heavy father, once the novelty of doing so had worn off, she told herself firmly. And when the divorce came through and he married Valerie Langton, she might not want a stepson who was already half her age.

Deciding to give Aunt Hannah tea in bed for a change, Abby dressed at once and went downstairs, and by the time she heard anyone stirring, she had the fire lighted, and the tea already made.

'What time is it?' exclaimed the old lady anxiously, as Abby carried the tray into her room, and her niece drew the curtains smilingly before turning to the bed.

'It's only a quarter past seven,' she said, 'but I thought you deserved a break. I've emptied the ashes and lit the fire, and if you tell me what you'd like for breakfast, I'll bring that upstairs, too.'

'Oh, Abby . . .' Hannah took her tea gratefully, levering herself up on her pillows. Somehow, seen in bed, she seemed so much frailer, so vulnerable, and Abby knew an aching pang for causing her any distress.

'I thought you'd like to know that I've got over my sulks,' she said determinedly. 'After all, I wanted to come here, didn't I? It was only Matthew—and Piers—that were stopping me. Well that's over now. We're here. And I'm going to do my best to see you don't suffer by it.'

'Suffer by it?' echoed Hannah faintly. 'My dear, I can't tell you how happy I am that you've decided to see it this way. You've made an old woman very happy. And to prove it, I'm going to get up and make your breakfast instead.'

Piers arrived soon after the breakfast dishes had been

cleared away. It was half past nine, and Matthew was outside, having eaten an enormous meal of cereal and scrambled eggs. Abby, hearing Piers' footsteps on the path as he walked round to the back of the house, felt herself stiffen automatically, and she couldn't deny the twinge of jealousy that gripped her when she heard how enthusiastically Matthew greeted his father.

'Look who's here,' he said, coming to the kitchen door. Then: 'Hey, is that your estate car at the gate? It's a Mercedes, isn't it? Can I go and look?'

'So long as you don't try to start the engine,' agreed Piers handing him the keys. 'Good morning, Abby,' he added, propping himself against the door frame. 'And you, Miss Caldwell. I trust you all had a good night's rest.'

Hannah bustled over to the cooker. 'Will you have a cup of coffee, Piers?' she suggested, lifting the kettle to test the amount of water inside. 'It's just instant, but you're perfectly welcome. We've just had breakfast, and——'

'As a matter of fact, I came to ask Abby if she'd care to come for a drive with me,' he declared smoothly, meeting Abby's startled gaze with narrow-eyed enquiry. 'We have to talk, and I have something I want to show her. You have no objection if we leave Matthew with you, have you, Miss Caldwell?'

'Of course not. Abby?' Hannah looked expectantly at her niece. 'Abby, is that all right with you?'

Abby squared her shoulders. 'We can talk here. We did before.'

'Matthew was asleep before,' retorted Piers straightening. 'Get your coat, or whatever it is you need to wear over what you've got on. The car's warm, you won't need anything much.'

Abby looked down at her jeans and cotton sweater. Then she looked up at him again. 'If you insist on this outing, then I'll get changed,' she said stiffly.

'Why? You look okay to me.' Piers, as usual, looked as if he had been poured into his clothes, and although he, too, was wearing denim slacks, they merely complemented the powerful length of his legs.

'If we're going somewhere——' she began reluctantly, only to find Piers regarding her mockingly.

'Nowhere of importance,' he assured her lazily. 'Just bring a jacket. I'll wait in the car.'

By the time Abby emerged from the cottage, Matthew was installed on the wall beside the garden gate, his drooping expression indicative of his disappointment in not accompanying them.

'Don't worry about him,' Piers remarked as Abby got into the car. 'He's got to learn not to take you for granted. He does, you know, and you're a fool to let him.'

'Oh, I'm a fool, all right,' agreed Abby bitterly, as he started the car and they drove away. 'I was a fool to let you organise my life for me. That was a pretty mean trick sending that man Shand to the hearing. I didn't need your assistance, I could have managed on my own.'

'Could you?' They were driving through the village now, and Piers raised his hand to various people as they waved a greeting. 'It seems to me you weren't making such a great job of it. I thought you were having difficulty controlling the boy.'

'What do you mean?' Abby turned to stare at him. 'Just because he had one brush with the police——'

'Not just one brush, Abby. One brush that you know about. God, he's an habitual absentee from school. He's been seen acting suspiciously in that store before. It's a miracle he's not been arrested before now. And I heard what happened while he was in the village. Rothside is a small place, Abby. People were only too eager to tell me what he got up to while he was here.'

'Is that why you're doing this? Because of what people might say?'

Piers' jaw hardened. 'You should know better than that, Abby.'

'Well, why are you doing it, then? You don't care about Matt—you never have. Why can't you leave us alone? I didn't ask for your assistance.'

'True.' Piers turned the estate car on to the Alnbury

road. 'Perhaps I just felt sorry for you. You are still my wife.'

Abby's hands curled into fists. 'I don't want your charity.'

'Matthew does.'

'That's a low thing to say!'

'But true.' Piers' tone was crisp. 'You were losing your job, Abby. You would probably have lost that flat as well. What local authority could allow you to bring up a child in those circumstances, particularly a child with Matthew's unstable history?'

Abby was cornered. He was right, but that didn't make it any easier to swallow. 'What are you saying?' she demanded, forcing a provocative note into her voice. 'That you did what you did for me, and not for Matt?'

'I don't know Matthew,' responded Piers quietly. 'As you persistently point out, I have ignored his existence for eleven years. But you are still my wife, Abby. It was our twelfth anniversary in August.'

'Of which we've spent precisely four months together,' Abby retorted.

'Four months?' Piers turned his head to look at her, his tawny eyes dark and impregnably guarded. 'Yes, I suppose that was the length of time you lived at the Manor. But our being together lasted much longer than that.'

Abby bent her head, shocked to find her knees were trembling. 'That was different. That was before—before your mother knew about us. You—you were going to marry Melanie Hastings. Our—our relationship was never meant to be taken seriously.'

'But it was.'

'It shouldn't have been.'

'Agreed.' Piers' harsh word of acquiescence silenced them both for a while, and not until they turned off the main road on to the road to Warkwick did Abby voice her curiosity:

'Where are we going?'

'To Warkwick,' said Piers steadily. 'There's a school there, Abbotsford—have you heard of it?'

Abby frowned. 'Isn't that where you went to school?'

'That's right.'

'It's a boarding school.'

'It's both,' Piers informed her evenly. 'I admit, most of the boys are boarders, but the headmaster is prepared to take day boys, if their parents prefer it.'

Abby did a double take. 'You mean—you're thinking Matt should go there?'

'Why not?'

'Why not?' Abby shook her head. 'You know why not. The fees must be phenomenal!'

'Oh, not as much as that,' replied Piers dryly. 'In the area of fifteen hundred a year——'

'Fifteen hundred!'

'—and the standard of teaching is first class.'

'I don't doubt it.' Abby shook her head. 'Piers, this is crazy!'

'Why is it crazy? Don't you want the boy to have a good education?'

'Well, yes—but, oh—Piers, you can't do this!'

'Why can't I? I can afford it.'

'That's not the point . . .'

'You object to my interference.'

Abby sighed. 'It's not necessary.'

'You'd rather he went to the comprehensive and took his chances with the rest of them?'

'In the normal way, yes.'

Piers expelled his breath noisily. 'Well, at least you admit this isn't quite a normal situation.'

'Matt may settle down at Alnbury——'

'And he may not.' They were approaching the village of Warkwick now, and Piers pulled the car off the road, parking it in the shade of a clump of fir trees. 'Abby,' he turned towards her, 'if Matthew hadn't been in trouble with the police, I wouldn't have suggested it, but in the circumstances it may be the best thing for him.'

'He'll know I can't afford it.'

'I know that.' Piers hesitated. 'Abby, it seems to me from what you've told me, and from the way Matthew

behaves, that what's really wrong with the boy is rooted
in the fact that he doesn't have a father. Or at least——'
this as Abby would have protested, '—a father who cares
about him.'

'He doesn't need a father,' muttered Abby tautly.
'We've managed okay——'

'Until now,' Piers interrupted flatly. 'Abby, admit it.
The kid's all mixed up. As he sees it, you left me because
we didn't get on. Not much of a reason for breaking up a
marriage.'

Abby held up her head. 'And are you going to tell him
the truth?'

'Not immediately, no.' Piers considered his words before
speaking them. 'That's why I intend to take him to the
Manor——'

'The Manor!'

'—and let him get to know Val properly.'

A sharp pain flowered in Abby's stomach at the casual
mention of his girl-friend. For a few minutes, she had
forgotten about the divorce, forgotten about Valerie
Langton, forgotten everything but their mutual desire to
do what was best for Matthew.

'And your mother?' she taunted, needing to expunge
her jealousy in some other way. 'What will she have to
say if you bring *my* son into her home? She never wanted
me there, goodness knows, and I won't allow her to hurt
Matt.'

'She won't hurt him.' Piers' mouth had tightened at
her mention of his mother's name. 'Believe it or not, my
mother never hated you. She was distressed when I jilted
Melanie, of course——'

'*Distressed!*'

'—but she accepted the fact that I was marrying you.
Even if she did suspect Tristan Oliver had a prior claim.'

Abby's pale face filled with hot colour. 'That was a
lie——'

'Oh, I admit, you were a virgin when I—well, when I
first made love to you.'

'When you *first*?' Abby knew she kept repeating the

things he said, but she couldn't help it. They were so unfair, and she had no weapons with which to fight him. 'Piers, I think you'd better take me back. We've had this kind of conversation before, and quite frankly I've heard enough.'

Piers shrugged, but he made no immediate move to start the car again. 'Tristan went to Canada, you know,' he said after a moment, as if they were simply indulging in casual conversation. 'I thought, at first, he'd gone after you.'

Abby said nothing, bending her head, the curtain of her hair falling forward to hide her expression.

'Did he come to see you?' Piers asked, with more insistence. 'Did he tell you what he was going to do? Why didn't you go with him? You can't deny that he was in love with you.'

Abby still said nothing, and as if growing impatient of her silence, Piers lifted his hand and looped her hair back behind her ear. She steeled herself not to flinch away from his touch, and then felt a shudder run through her when he said huskily: 'You haven't changed, you know. You're still as desirable as you were fifteen years ago. There, does that shock you? I saw you—and wanted you—when you weren't even sixteen.'

Abby lifted her head. 'Is this a new approach?' she inquired tensely. 'Another form of persuasion? I don't need you to tell me I'm desirable, Piers. I'm not. I'm a harassed housewife of almost thirty years of age, and I know, without any self-deception, that I look it!'

'You don't look any older than Val,' retorted Piers, swinging round in his seat abruptly and turning the ignition. 'I'll show you the school, then we'll go back. You can make up your mind over the weekend. If you're agreeable, we'll come and see the headmaster next week, before I go to Germany.'

'You're going to Germany?' Abby couldn't prevent the automatic question.

'Just for a week. Val and I met a German count and his wife when we were skiing in Austria earlier in the year. They live in the Rhine valley, and they've invited us to visit them while some local beer festival is going on.'

'I see.' Abby despised herself for the feeling of stark jealousy his words evoked. 'That should be—interesting. I suppose—Miss Langton is going with you.'

'She is.' Piers glanced her way. 'This is the school. What do you think of it?'

Abbotsford was an old school, the buildings rambling and ivy-covered, but even from a distance it had a charm that Abby could not ignore. Surrounded by a wall and a belt of trees, lush green playing fields stretched towards the River Coquet, its dappled waters forming a boundary on the eastern side of the property.

'Well?'

Piers was waiting for her reaction, and on impulse Abby pushed open her door and got out of the car. 'It looks—ideal,' she murmured, aware of him getting out behind her and following her across to the tall iron gates. 'How old were you when you came here? I suppose you were a boarder.'

'Not to begin with,' Piers replied, coming to stand beside her. 'I was only eight when I started at Abbotsford. I was a day boy, too, to begin with. Later, I became a boarder. It suited my parents better that way.'

Abby tried to imagine Piers at eight. She supposed he must have been much like Matthew at that age, if not in looks, then certainly in temperament. Matthew had been such a delightful, lovable child.

Lovable! Abby cast a surreptitious glance up at her husband. It was not the sort of adjective she should have associated with Piers. Not after what had happened; not after the way he had treated her. And yet, like Matthew, he could be so charming when he chose, and an involuntary shiver ran over her when she realised the path her thoughts were taking.

'You're cold!' He could be thoughtful, too, and Abby's senses stirred with unwilling remembrance when he put a casual arm about her waist to guide her back to the car. 'Come on. You don't want to catch a cold.'

'I'm all right.' But Abby's voice was breathy, and Piers looked quickly down at her as they crossed the grassy verge.

'Perhaps I should have let you change after all,' he remarked a little roughly, opening her door. 'Do you have anything on under this sweater? Your body feels chilled.'

Abby slid hastily into the car, and she had recovered herself somewhat by the time he had circled the bonnet to get in beside her. 'I wasn't cold until I got out of the car,' she murmured, hoping he would let it drop, but Piers' eyes were disturbing as they searched her nervous face.

'I guess you're remembering that afternoon we walked to High Tor, aren't you?' he demanded, his lean face intent. 'Do you remember the mist coming down, and how we were both chilled to the bone?'

'Piers, let's go——'

'In a minute.' Piers hadn't finished his story. 'The peel tower's still there, you know. Or at least, the remains of it is. I doubt if anyone's touched the ashes of our fire, or disturbed the bed we made for ourselves——'

'What are you trying to do, Piers?' Abby's cry was incensed, and his dark face grew sombre as he met her tremulous gaze.

'I don't know,' he said harshly. 'Maybe I'm trying to discover the reasons why everything went wrong.' He made a derisive sound. 'You always were a disrupting creature.'

'I didn't ask you to marry me,' Abby retorted, wrapping her arms tightly about her, and Piers gave a wry nod of acknowledgement as he started the car.

'No, you didn't,' he conceded. 'But you were bloody glad I did. What problems would you have had with Matthew, I wonder, if he'd been illegitimate as well?'

'Probably none,' Abby countered, stung by his malicious challenge, and thereafter they did not speak again until Matthew himself met them at the cottage gate.

On Saturday, Piers took Matthew to meet his grandmother.

Abby had not wanted to let him go when Piers first broached the subject, over the cup of coffee Hannah had insisted on him having after their return from Abbotsford. But Matthew's own enthusiasm, and the warning glances Hannah cast in her direction, persuaded her not to make a fuss, and after Piers had gone and they were alone, her aunt applauded her decision.

'They are his family, after all,' she pointed out, when Abby voiced her objections. 'And let's face it, Piers could enforce his rights if you chose to be awkward.'

It was infuriatingly true. Unless she played into Piers' hands and denounced Matthew as his son, there was no real opposition she could raise; and as Piers *was* the boy's father, he had every right to share his affections.

Nevertheless, it wasn't easy to be enthusiastic when Matthew came back full of excitement and eager to tell her all that had happened. He was like a small boy again, and Hannah exchanged a knowing look with Abby when he mentioned his grandmother for the first time.

'She's quite old,' he said. 'And she can't walk far because of her leg.'

'Her leg?' Hannah looked at him askance, and Matthew giggled.

'I mean, she has arthritis,' he explained, helping himself to one of the scones his mother had made that afternoon and munching happily. 'That's why she doesn't ride much any more. But she still keeps horses, and Dad showed me a pony he says I can learn to ride.'

Dad! Abby drew a deep breath. How casually he said it. But how had Mrs Roth really reacted to her grandson? And would Matthew have noticed if she had been terse or offhand?

'A pony,' Hannah was saying admiringly. 'Aren't you the lucky one! And does it have a name, this pony? Or have you to think of that as well?'

'Oh, no.' Matthew shook his head. 'His name's Hazel, after one of the rabbits in *Watership Down*. That's a book by a man called Richard Adams,' he confided. 'Dad says I should read it, and he's going to get me a copy.'

Abby forced herself to smile. 'So you enjoyed yourself?'

'Oh, yes, it's a lovely place. I don't know why you didn't like it, Mum. The rooms are so big, and the furniture's so grand!' He sighed. 'We had tea, you know, in the drawing room. That Miss Langton was there. She's all right, I suppose. A bit snobby, but I think she was trying to please Dad by being friendly.'

How perceptive of him to notice, Abby thought, somewhat relieved. At least he hadn't been entirely blinded by his surroundings. But did that mean Mrs Roth had passed the test?

For the rest of the weekend, Abby had to steel herself to listen to various other items of interest Matthew thought she might like to hear. It was obvious the events of Saturday had engraved themselves on his memory, and she had to accept that the days when his father's name was never mentioned were lost to her for ever.

Dr Willis came to see his patient on Monday morning, and he greeted Abby with evident enthusiasm.

'So you came back, after all,' he said, coming downstairs after examining Hannah in her bedroom. 'I hope you're going to stay this time.'

'I hope so, too.' Abby indicated the kettle. 'Will you have a cup of coffee? I was just making one.'

'Could I refuse?' Sean grinned, and lounged familiarly into a chair by the fire. 'Where's the boy, then? I was looking forward to meeting him.'

'Oh, he's just gone to the stores for Aunt Hannah,' said Abby, feeling herself colouring. 'I suppose you've heard about Matthew. I expect it's common knowledge in the village.'

'I heard that he was Piers Roth's son,' Sean admitted, 'but that didn't surprise me. Should it?'

Abby frowned. 'Well——'

'I guessed you were related. The names,' he explained easily. 'But anyway, what business is it of anyone else's? In my book, a person's private affairs are their own.'

'Thank you,' Abby smiled, and then Hannah reappeared to endorse the invitation her niece had already offered.

Matthew returned while they were drinking their coffee, and to Abby's disconcertment, Piers was with him. 'Dad gave me a lift,' he said, giving Sean a speculative look. 'He wants to speak to you, Mum. About the school he wants me to go to.'

Abby gave her husband a frosty look. 'You've discussed it with Matthew?'

'I mentioned it,' he agreed flatly, returning Sean's greeting with chilly courtesy. 'How nice to have a practice that takes care of itself, Willis. Does your answering service know where you are?'

'Dr Willis has been attending me,' declared Hannah shortly, showing her indignation at Piers' incivility. 'Finish your coffee, doctor. Don't let Mr Roth frighten you away.'

'I assure you, I'm not frightened, Miss Caldwell,' Sean replied firmly, getting to his feet and handing her his empty cup. 'But it is time I was leaving. Nice to have met you, Matthew. Cheerio, Roth. G'bye—Abby. I hope I see you again soon.'

The atmosphere was electric after Sean had left, but Piers chose to ignore it. 'Well, Abby?' he said, his voice only a couple of degrees warmer than when he had addressed Sean Willis. 'Have you made up your mind?'

'You appear to have made it up for me,' she responded tautly. 'Matt, what do you want to do? Do you want to go to this boy's school your father is talking about? Or would you rather go to Alnbury?'

She guessed what his answer would be, and she wasn't disappointed. 'I'd like to go to Dad's old school,' he declared, looking up at Piers. 'Can I come and see it? Is it very big?'

'It's not big at all,' said Piers, transferring his attention back to Abby. 'I believe it caters for four hundred boys, that's all. As for going to see it, I suggest your mother and I make a preliminary visit to see Mr Grant, the headmaster, tomorrow morning, and then we'll arrange for you to go and look round.'

'When will I start there?'

Matthew sounded eager, but Abby suspected his enthusiasm might not last long after he discovered how much homework he would be expected to do.

'After Christmas,' Piers answered now. 'Abby, I made a provisional appointment for ten o'clock in the morning. Is that all right with you?'

'Does it matter?' Abby couldn't help feeling bitter. Piers had arranged it all once again without consulting her. Just because she had seemed impressed with its appearance, he had gone ahead and made his plans. And unless she wanted to hurt Matthew, she had to go along with them.

CHAPTER SEVEN

It was raining on Tuesday morning, a persistent steady downpour, that caused the clouds to lower ominously above the village, and cast a grey curtain over everything.

Abby had had some difficulty in deciding what to wear. A suit was obviously the most adaptable, but her suits were hardly fashionable, and they had seen many weeks of wear in Trevor's office. Eventually, she decided on a cowl-necked dress of cherry silk jersey she had bought a year ago to attend a professional luncheon with Trevor. It wasn't real silk jersey, just a clever facsimile, but it flattered the rounded swell of her breasts and clung lovingly to the line of her hips. With it she wore the only jacket she possessed, a plain black corded velvet, that made a dark contrast with the silvery lightness of her hair.

Piers made no comment on her appearance when he came to collect her in the Daimler. He merely took the umbrella Aunt Hannah had given her to walk from the cottage to the car and stowed it in the boot before levering his length beside her. In a dark grey three-piece suit that accentuated his dark colouring, he looked cool and detached, but Abby couldn't prevent the flutter of awareness that accompanied her tight nod of greeting.

Mr Grant turned out to be a charming man. In his early fifties, he epitomised everything a parent hoped for in a headmaster, combining a genuine liking for children with a sternness that still found room for humour.

'Your husband has explained the circumstances of the situation to me, Mrs Roth,' he told Abby sympathetically. 'Matthew, I'm sure, will benefit from having the attention of both parents again.'

'Yes.' Abby forced a smile, but she wondered what Piers

had told him. Matthew had never known the luxury of having both parents' attention until now, and she hoped that the experience would not prove too much for him.

Outside again, Abby breathed more freely, hurrying to get in the car out of the rain. Piers had offered to bring the umbrella, but she said it wasn't necessary, even though she was panting by the time she had run to the Daimler.

'You're soaked!' exclaimed Piers, brushing the drops of water from his own jacket. The material of his had not absorbed the wet as hers had, and she could feel its moistness creeping through to her skin. 'Take your jacket off,' he advised, reaching for the ignition. 'There's no point in catching a chill. Drop it in the back for the present. It's warm enough in here not to need it.'

Abby hesitated, but deciding he was probably right, she slipped the jacket off her shoulders and removed it. It was a relief to be free of its cloying wetness, and she rubbed her arms abrasively, restoring a feeling of warmth.

'We'll look round the school next week, when we bring Matthew to see it,' Piers added, as they drove away. 'You are happy with the arrangements, aren't you? You're not going to hold Matthew's eagerness against me?'

'I suppose not.' Abby tucked her damp hair behind her ears. 'There's not much point now, is there? I'm committed.'

'Not necessarily,' said Piers levelly. 'I can always call the whole thing off. If you really feel Matthew would be better off at the school in Alnbury, I'm prepared to waive any objections I may have.'

Abby sighed. 'You know I wouldn't do that.'

'Do I?'

Abby bent her head. 'There's just one thing . . .'

'Well?'

'How will Matt get to school? I don't suppose there's a school bus.'

'I thought I'd have a word with the Crofts,' replied Piers, slowing for a road junction. 'Their eldest son is a day boy, and I believe Sarah runs him to school in the

morning and collects him every afternoon. I'm sure she'd
have no objection to picking up Matthew on her way.'

'Sarah Croft?' Abby queried. Sarah had been one of
the few friends she had had when she and Piers had got
married.

'I thought you'd approve of her,' remarked Piers dryly.
'Robert, her boy, will be about six months younger than
Matthew.'

Abby inclined her head. 'Sarah Croft,' she murmured
again. 'It will be nice to see Sarah again.'

'She wrote to you, didn't she? After you left Rothside?
She once told me that. She also told me you didn't reply.'

'No.' Abby drew an unsteady breath. 'I didn't think
there was much point.'

'Why not?'

'Oh—the Crofts were really your friends, not mine.
And—well, I suppose I was—embarrassed.'

'Embarrassed!'

'Don't pretend you don't understand.' Abby's voice was
husky. 'How could I go on being friendly with Sarah,
when no one knew about the baby?'

Piers gave her a sidelong look. 'Why didn't you tell
her? I've no doubt, knowing Sarah as I do, she'd have
taken your part.'

'I didn't want anyone to take my part,' retorted Abby
wearily. 'I just wanted to—forget it.'

'Forget me, you mean?'

Abby shrugged. 'If you like.'

'And did you?'

'Yes.' Abby was adamant.

'Completely?'

Abby turned her head and looked at him. 'As you forgot
me!'

'I didn't forget you, Abby.'

'But you didn't want to remember me, did you?'

Piers lifted his shoulders. 'I had reason, didn't I?'

'You believed you did.'

'Yes.' He paused. 'You didn't answer my questions.'

'What question?'

'I asked if you forgot me completely.'

Abby moistened her lips. 'It isn't easy to forget someone you hate.'

She heard his swift intake of breath. 'Do you still? Hate me, I mean?'

Abby turned to stare out of the window at the driving rain. She wanted to say that yes, she still hated him, more now than before, but she knew it wouldn't be true. Since she had seen him again, since she had unwillingly allowed him to become involved in her life, her feelings had changed, become less resolute. Where once she had been absolutely sure that she could never forgive him for the way he had humiliated her, now she was wavering, her convictions shaken. Time, like a corrosive, had eaten away at her hatred, and being with him again, allowing all the old attraction to pull at her senses, she was rapidly losing the will to oppose him.

'Where are we going?' she asked abruptly, as she came out of her reverie to find he had turned away from the village. 'This isn't the way to Rothside.' She hesitated. 'It's the private road that leads to the Manor.'

'That's right.' Piers cast a swift look in her direction, his attention concentrated on avoiding the deep pools of water that were rapidly gathering in the lane. 'I thought we might have lunch at home, just for old times' sake. What do you say?'

Abby's nerves quivered. 'Have lunch at the Manor?' she echoed faintly. 'With your mother?' Her lips twisted. 'Somehow I don't think she'd approve.'

'She's not at home,' replied Piers flatly. 'She's gone into Newcastle with Aunt Isabel for a day's shopping. She won't be back until later this afternoon.'

Abby knew a strangely familiar feeling of *déjà vu*. Piers' words had brought back unwanted memories of their first illicit meetings, illicit, because his mother would have prevented them if she could. There had been days like this before, days when Mrs Roth had left them alone, days before she had seen Abby as any threat to her carefully-nurtured plans.

It had begun so innocently, or so Abby had thought. After all, she had been only sixteen, and the job at the Manor had been her first term of employment. She had not been unaware of the opposite sex, but she had never met anyone like Piers before, and although she had been attracted to him, she had never imagined he might be attracted to her.

Piers had taken over the running of the estate when his father died. Because the elder Mr Roth had been ill for some time before his death, the affairs of the estate had been left in the hands of his agent, and although he had done his best, things had been allowed to slide. Piers had still been at university at that time, and the agents had been unable to take arbitrary decisions without recourse to a higher authority. In consequence, when Piers came home, there was already a stack of work waiting for him. In addition to which, his father's secretary, who had worked at the Manor for more than twenty years, left to look after an invalid mother, and when the position was advertised, Abby had applied.

She had not expected to get the post. There were other, more experienced applicants. But Piers had insisted he wanted someone he could mould to his own requirements, and not until afterwards did she discover he had had other reasons for choosing her.

But to begin with, Abby had only been relieved to have found employment so close to home. Most of the young people she had gone to school with had had to go into Alnbury or Newcastle to find work, while she was able to cycle the two and a half miles to the Manor. It saved bus fares, and meant she could give Aunt Hannah almost all her salary.

They were happy days, so happy. Thinking about them now, Abby sighed. Working with Piers, accompanying him when he drove about the estate, she soon learned all there was to know about property valuation and land management. She also began to appreciate the problems he faced when trying to maintain a good relationship with his tenants. There was so much petty bickering between tenants, so many ways in which the landlord could be accused of favouring one and not the other; and Piers had to try and steer a central course, while Abby could see that some tenants deserved a fairer deal than others.

Piers used to discuss his problems with Abby, welcoming her opinion, and gradually their discussions moved into more personal areas. He told her about his time at the university, and she told him about her parents, and how Aunt Hannah had looked after her when her father had been killed. He was easy to talk to, and he really seemed interested in what she had to say. Their conversations removed all the barriers between them, and Abby started to forget who he was and how disapproving his family would be if they discovered how familiar she had become.

It was about this time that Tristan Oliver invited her to go with him to a teenage dance in Alnbury. They could go on the bus, he said, and his father would come and pick them up afterwards. Tristan was seventeen and learning to drive, but he had not yet passed his test, though his boast was that when he did, his father was going to buy him a car of his own.

Encouraged by Aunt Hannah, Abby had accepted his invitation, and had mentioned it to Piers in passing. She had told him most things in those days, and although she had had little belief that he would care one way or the other, she had, perhaps subconsciously, wanted to show that she was not unattractive to boys of her own age.

She was shocked, therefore, when she emerged from the hall with Tristan and his father, to encounter Piers waiting outside. 'I had some business to attend to in Alnbury,' he told Mr Oliver smoothly, 'and as taking Abby home is less out of my way than yours, I thought I'd relieve you of that responsibility.'

Tristan's father had been surprised, obviously, but as Piers' explanation was quite reasonable, he did not argue. The Olivers were not tenants of the Roths, they owned their own farm, and as Piers had said, it would be taking them well out of their way to take Abby home. In consequence, a few minutes later Abby found herself installed in the front seat of Piers' station wagon, with Piers beside her driving back to Rothside.

'You didn't mind, did you?' Piers asked, as soon as the lights of Alnbury market square fell away behind them.

Abby considered this before replying, and then she said: 'You didn't really have any business in Alnbury, did you?'

'No.' Piers was honest.

Abby moved her shoulders. 'You came to meet me.' It was a statement, not a question.

'Yes.'

'You shouldn't have.'

Piers gave her a sidelong glance. 'I know.'

Abby caught her breath. 'Piers——'

'No, don't say anything,' he commanded, his jaw taut. 'Just let's leave it at that, shall we?'

Abby's lips parted. 'If that's what you want to do,' she replied unsteadily.

'If that's what I want to do?' Piers stood on his brakes, bringing the station wagon to a skidding halt that almost threw her through the windscreen before turning to her. 'It's not what I want to do, Abby,' he said, in a voice that seemed to tear a layer of skin from her. 'You must know what I want to do, and you have every right to despise me for it.'

Abby quivered. 'I don't—despise you, Piers,' she breathed, realising with sudden insight that this was the real reason she enjoyed being with him, that this was the true extent of her feelings for him. It wasn't just that he was a likeable person to work for—to be with. It wasn't even his kindness or his consideration when she had problems. It was the underlying knowledge of her attraction for him, and the realisation that she wanted more from this relationship than she had any right to expect.

'Abby?' He was staring at her tautly, and even in the dim light from the dash she was aware of the intensity of his gaze. 'Abby, don't play games with me. I'm not one of your boy-friends; I'm not Tristan Oliver.'

'I know.'

Abby moved her head helplessly, and he lifted his hand suddenly to brush the silky fringe back from her forehead. She had worn her hair longer in those days and for the dance she had secured it with a leather clip. Now she felt him release the clip, and her hair fell forward, a silky curtain that reached half to her waist.

'What do you know, I wonder?' he muttered, his mouth twisting sensually, and Abby's nerves jangled in anticipation of its touch.

'Not—not a lot,' she admitted, conscious of his body, conscious of him as she had never been before—and equally, conscious of her own inexperience.

'I shouldn't find out,' he added, his voice thickening in spite of himself. 'You're too young——'

Abby caught her breath. 'Don't say that!'

'Why not? It's true.' But Piers' gaze still impaled hers, and his hand had moved from her nape to stroke the downy softness of her cheek.

Almost involuntarily, Abby turned her head so that her lips brushed his palm. It was an instinctive thing to do, an insistent desire to make some response, however small, and its results were electrifying. With a muffled oath, Piers rubbed his thumb abrasively across her mouth, parting her lips and exploring the softness within. Then, before she had time to get used to this new and strangely intimate invasion, his thumb was withdrawn and his mouth took its place.

As she remembered that kiss now, Abby's senses tingled. She might not have been prepared for the raw adult passion Piers had shown her, but she had been a willing pupil. And more than that, she had been shown the untried sensuality of her own nature, that equalled his in urgency when he would have drawn away. Instead, she had linked her arms about his neck, her eager fingers clutching the hair that grew there, her mouth opening like a flower to the hungry passion of his . . .

'Well?'

Realising Piers was still waiting for her answer, Abby

moved her head in a negative gesture, glancing back over her shoulder, as if somehow she could see the cottage. 'Aunt Hannah is expecting me,' she exclaimed. 'She'll worry if we don't go back. Particularly when the weather is so bad.'

'Send her a message,' said Piers tautly. 'I'll get Jerrold to take it. She won't worry if she knows you're with me. Whatever her feelings, she still regards me as a gentleman.'

'Does she?' Abby's tongue circled her upper lip. 'I wonder.'

'Abby, please.' Piers drew a deep breath. 'Indulge me.'

'Why should I?'

Piers sighed. 'For old times' sake, what else?'

'And Miss Langton?'

'Val isn't involved here,' he retorted roughly. 'This is between you and me, Abby. Hell, I've already written to my solicitor about the divorce. This may be our last chance to talk as man and wife.'

Abby bent her head. The rain outside seemed to be conspiring against her. Trapped in the car with Piers, unable to get out and walk, even had she wanted to because of the terrible weather, she was being compelled to consider his invitation almost against her will.

It was all so devastatingly familiar. She didn't want to remember what had been between her and Piers in those early days, but she couldn't seem to help it. Like a video-tape it was unrolling there before her eyes, and although she fought against it, she could not deny the physical effect it was having on her.

The memory of the first occasion Piers had made love to her came back in spine-shuddering detail, and she struggled to evade its insidious enchantment. But without much success. It was incredible that something that had happened almost fourteen years ago should still have the power to disturb her, but it did.

Their relationship—hers and Piers'—had developed so swiftly. From the beginning they had both known it was

only a matter of time before the frenzied kisses they exchanged incited a deeper commitment. Piers was not a
womaniser, but he was not without sexual experience, and
while his mouth searched the eager softness of hers, his
hands made their own exploration. At first, Abby had
demurred, the things Aunt Hannah had taught her
arousing a troubled voice of conscience. But gradually,
her own body's needs overwhelmed her caution, and she
welcomed his hands upon her with an eagerness he could
not withstand.

They were young, and in love, and during the long
days of that first summer Abby worked at the Manor, the
atmosphere between them became electric. They were too
much in one another's company, too much alone; and
when the inevitable happened, it seemed a natural exten-
sion of their need for one another. She wondered now
how Mrs Roth had not seen what was happening under
her eyes, but perhaps because she never saw Abby as anything else but one of the 'village girls' she expected Piers
to do the same.

It was a hot summer evening, Abby recalled unwillingly. She had been working later than usual, helping
Mrs Roth address the envelopes for a garden party
which was to be held at the Manor the following week.
It was in aid of some charity association, she remembered, and she had been willing enough to help Piers'
mother, as Piers himself had gone to the races with some
friends.

But it was while they were addressing the envelopes
that Mrs Roth made her announcement: 'Maybe this time
next year, we'll be addressing the invitations to Piers'
wedding,' she remarked, with smug complacency. 'Dear
Melanie! Such a lovely girl. And what an admirable wife
she'll make.'

Abby had known at once who she meant. Melanie
Hastings had been seen frequently at the Manor in recent
months. Her parents were close friends of Mrs Roth, and
Abby had foolishly assumed that that was the only reason
Melanie was there. Now, it appeared, she was wrong, and

her hand had shaken infuriatingly as she struggled to complete her task.

Piers arrived home just as Abby was leaving, and encountering her wheeling her bicycle into the courtyard, he had stepped in front of her. 'Wait,' he said, his eyes dark and disturbing, 'I'll take you home. Just give me a minute to get the Range Rover.'

'No, thanks.' Abby was terse. 'I can manage. Goodnight—Mr Roth. I'll see you tomorrow.'

'*Abby!*' Piers had detained her then, his hand on her arm. 'What's with this *Mr* Roth?' He frowned, as his brain sought for a solution. 'What has my mother been saying to you?'

'Your mother?' Abby's green eyes flashed fire. 'What could she say to me? Except perhaps that you're getting married next year?' And shaking off his hand, she had jumped on her bicycle and ridden away.

He overtook her long before she reached the boundary of his family's property, slewing the Range Rover across the road, and forcing her to stop.

'Get in,' he commanded violently, wrenching the bicycle from her hands and flinging it into the back of the vehicle. And when she had done so, he vaulted in beside her and regarded her with a hard, yet impassioned, malevolence.

'Isn't it true, then?' she had asked him, maintaining a chilly façade, even while she was churning up inside with emotion. But Piers had not answered her. He had thrown the Range Rover into gear and accelerated away, tossing her only a savage look as he turned off the road and into the trees.

The shadows were lengthening when Piers had brought the Range Rover to a halt, overlooking the rippling expanse of the trout lake, that occupied several acres at the eastern boundary of the property. It was quite a beauty spot, the reed-edged waters set about with trees that grew thickly on the higher slopes that surrounded it. But Abby knew he had not brought her here to look at the view, and she started violently when he thrust open his door and climbed out.

He had shed the jacket of the suit he had worn to go to the race meeting, and she watched as he walked to the edge of the lake, to stand staring broodingly out across the water. His bronze silk shirt rippled in the slight breeze that blew off the water, and when he turned, she saw it was unbuttoned half down his chest.

He walked back to where she was sitting, setting her heart pounding when he wrenched open her door. 'Don't you trust me?' he demanded, his gesture inviting her to join him, but Abby stayed where she was.

'Should I?' she queried, gulping in a breath of air, and with a twisting of his expression he thrust his hands beneath her and lifted her bodily out of the vehicle.

'Probably not,' he declared huskily, looking down at her with smouldering eyes. 'The way I feel right now, you have every reason to be afraid of me.'

'Then take me home,' she exclaimed, steeling herself not to respond to the urgent possession of his gaze. She had not forgotten that he had still not denied her accusation, and indignation vied with fascination as her hands struggled to push him away.

But all he did was to let her put her feet to the ground. And as her limbs slid down his body, she felt the arousal he intended her to feel. It was not the first time she had aroused him. It was not the first time she had felt the hardening muscles of his thighs surging against her. But this time it was different, this time he did not push her away, and her own inflamed senses made her arch her body towards his.

His hands slid down her back, settling on her hips and drawing her more firmly against him. Then his mouth sought the breathless parting of hers and her resistance ebbed beneath the hungry passion of his kiss.

He kissed her many times, the long, soul-destroying kisses he had been denying himself for some weeks now. Ever since they both realised the danger of emotions inflamed to burning point, they had avoided exacerbating an already volatile situation, but suddenly his control had snapped and raw need had taken its place. He was hungry for her, they were hungry for one another, and the thrusting urgency of his desire became an irresistible temptation.

There was grass beneath their feet, and Piers drew her down on to it, his hands separating her shirt from the waistband of her skirt, his fingers seeking and finding the throbbing fullness of her breast. Abby didn't try to stop him, she was too intent on relieving him of his shirt, and she caught her tongue between her teeth when the rough hardness of his chest crushed hers.

'Someone might come,' she breathed, when his naked body moved upon hers, but Piers seemed not to care.

'Let them,' he muttered thickly, his mouth ravaging the already swollen sweetness of her mouth. 'Just don't ask me to stop, Abby, because I can't.'

'I won't,' she whispered, even though she tensed when the pulsating strength of his manhood sought entry to her body.

'Don't fight it,' he advised, holding her eyes with his as he took possession of her, and stifled the agonised cry she uttered beneath the parted intimacy of his mouth.

It hurt. For a few moments, that was all Abby could think of, and not even the tender caress of his hands could assuage the raw pain he had inflicted. And then he started to move and she thought he was going to leave her, and her trembling limbs encircled him, holding him even closer.

'Abby . . .' he groaned, her passionate nature almost driving him to the brink of insanity as he struggled to hold himself back. But it was too late. He spent himself helplessly, burying his face in the silken softness of her hair as his shuddering limbs convulsed.

Abby lay there quietly, content in the knowledge that she had pleased him, and not until he propped himself up on one hand to look at her did the realisation of what had happened bring the hot colour to her face. His eyes were dark and liquid, his gaze glazed and caressing as it moved possessively over her. Then, with a sigh, he bent his head to kiss her, and her slim arms wound impulsively about his neck.

'Was—was it all right?' she breathed in his ear, when he released her mouth to seek the scented hollow of her neck, and he made a sound half of anguish, half of amusement.

'Oh, Abby,' he muttered, his hand sliding sensuously over her breast and the slim curve of her thigh. 'Abby—you were beautiful! So beautiful! But I'll do better next time.'

'Next time?' Abby caught her breath, and as she did so she felt his body stirring inside her.

'Now,' he agreed huskily, sliding his hands beneath her hips and arching her body to meet his.

'Oh, no.' Abby shook her head. 'I mean—you can't——'

'I'm afraid I can,' he told her, with rough gentleness. 'Only this time it will be different, I promise you.'

And it was. Even now, Abby could remember the flowering delight he had generated inside her. She had had no idea what to expect, what kind of 'different' he meant. But urgently, insistently, she had felt the expanding need for a fulfilment only he was capable of supplying, a wanting, a yearning, a striving to get closer, even closer to him, until the urgent, throbbing rhythm of their bodies reached an unbelievable climax. She had moved with him, had responded with every nerve and sinew of her ardent nature, and when that peak of ecstasy was reached and she fell away into nothingness, she did not recognise the cry she heard as issuing from her own lips . . .

CHAPTER EIGHT

'ABBY . . .'

She realised abruptly that the car had stopped on the forecourt before the Manor, and Piers had turned in his seat and was regarding her with scarcely concealed impatience. How long had he been sitting there, waiting for her to say something? she wondered, her colour deepening becomingly, as she viewed the disturbing prospect that he could read her thoughts.

'I—I can't,' she said now, the awareness of her own vulnerability making her shake her head almost in panic. 'No, Piers, take me back. I must go back. Besides,' she forced a note of derision into her voice, 'what if your mother came back and found us? Can you imagine how she would react to that situation?'

Piers' mouth thinned. 'I don't care how my mother would react,' he told her harshly. 'I'm thirty-seven now, Abby. Quite old enough to make my own decisions, and to offer my own invitations. Rothside Manor belongs to me, did you know? It became mine on my thirtieth birthday.' He pulled a wry face. 'My father's old-fashioned belief that by then I'd be married with a family of my own. He and Mother intended to retire to the villa at Antibes. Unfortunately, it didn't happen that way. My father was dead before you even came here, and Mother is much happier playing lady of the Manor than retiring.'

Abby bent her head. 'Why are you telling me this?'

'Because I want you to have lunch with me. For God's sake, Abby, is it so much to ask? All right, so you've got nothing to thank me for. At least let's part with civility, even if we couldn't live together that way.'

Abby drew a deep breath, looking through the streaming window to where Malton, the butler, was hovering on the porch, holding an umbrella. 'What—what will the staff say?'

'They'll probably tell my mother,' said Piers laconically. 'Do you care?' He shook his head. 'Come on, Abby. A couple of hours, that's all I'm asking.' His mouth tightened. 'Or would you rather take tea with Dr Willis?'

Abby gazed at him indignantly. 'You were very rude to Dr Willis.'

'Abby!'

'Oh—all right.' Abby gave in. 'But I mustn't stay long. Matthew will be dying to hear what happened at the school.'

'Matthew can wait,' said Piers flatly, and thrusting open his door, he summoned the butler to fetch the umbrella.

If Malton, or Mrs James, who had been housekeeper at the manor for more than twenty years, or Jerrold, who took charge of the horses, and who was despatched to explain Abby's whereabouts to her aunt, thought it strange that Piers should have brought his estranged wife to lunch at the Manor, they knew better than to comment upon it. Nevertheless, Abby was aware of the housekeeper's shrewd consideration as she showed her to one of the first floor bathrooms, a feat she could have performed herself had she not felt obliged to humour the woman.

'Nice to see you at the Manor again, Mrs Piers,' she remarked politely, lingering while her visitor combed her hair. She had always addressed Abby as Mrs Piers, to distinguish her from the elder Mrs Roth.

'It's nice to be here, Mrs James,' Abby replied, rather dishonestly, turning away from the mirror. Being at the manor was not *nice*, it was nerve-racking, and she wondered how she could have been foolish enough to allow Piers to persuade her.

Lunch was served in the family dining room. The family dining room was so-called because it was considerably smaller than the formal dining room, but nevertheless, its maroon silk walls and oblong polished table were intimidating enough for someone used to a cottage kitchen, and Abby remembered how nervous she had been in the first few weeks of their marriage.

They ate at one end of the table, sitting at right angles to each other, and served by a young maid who Abby had never seen before. Her name was Susan and she smiled at Piers a lot, reminding Abby irresistibly of the way she had been attracted to him. After all, she had been just like Susan, one of the village girls, infatuated by the fascination of an older man. Only Piers had been much younger in those days, only seven years older than she was, and he had returned her feelings—or she thought he had.

The meal was delicious. A fragrant consommé was followed by a supreme of chicken with rice, and to finish there was a raspberry fool. However, Abby's appetite had been depleted by the unwilling familiarity of her surroundings, and although Piers appeared to be enjoying his wine, his plate returned to the kitchen scarcely touched.

Conversation throughout the meal was stilted, primarily because of its being overheard, first by the maid and then by Mrs James, ostensibly come to clear the table, but really to find out if everything had been satisfactory.

'You didn't eat a lot, Mr Roth,' she observed, with the informality of long service. 'I wondered if the chicken was to your liking.'

'The chicken was fine, Mrs James,' Piers assured her, getting to his feet and moving round the table to draw back Abby's chair. 'I expect the weather has depressed my appetite. Did Jerrold deliver the message to Miss Caldwell?'

'Yes, sir. He was back some time ago. Will you be wanting Hedley to take Mrs—Mrs Roth home?'

'No, thank you, that won't be necessary,' he replied, as Abby rose stiffly to her feet. 'I'll be taking Mrs Roth back to the village. Thank you, Mrs James.'

The small dining room opened into a larger drawing room, and although Abby would have preferred to use the other door which led into the hall and thus make her departure that much more imminent, Piers stood aside for her to precede him into the drawing room. With Mrs James watching, she had little choice but to obey, and she passed him quickly, much too aware of his deliberate appraisal.

'I have to go,' she said, when the door was closed, but Piers merely indicated the tray of coffee cooling on the table by the couch.

'Not yet,' he said, indicating that she should take charge of the cups, and with a gesture of helplessness she subsided on to the Regency-striped cushions.

'Tell me,' he said, taking the cup she handed him and putting it half impatiently aside. 'When Matthew was a baby, how did you manage to support both him and yourself? You would take nothing from me, as you've pointed out. So how did you do it?'

Abby hesitated. 'You mean—did I resort to the supreme sacrifice?' she asked ironically, and his face darkened with colour.

'No, that was not what I meant,' he retorted harshly. 'I simply wanted to know how you lived.'

Abby shrugged, feeling on surer ground. 'I applied for social security,' she said. 'Supplementary benefit. I'm sure you know all about it. You'd be amazed how resourceful a person can be when they're desperate.'

'You had no need to be desperate,' Piers exclaimed savagely. 'For God's sake, Abby, the money was there. Why didn't you use it?'

'For another man's child?' Abby found she could be cruel too. 'Oh, come on, Piers, I had some pride left. You were not going to deprive me of that as—as well as everything else.'

Piers paced across the floor, turning every now and then to look at her. 'And when the child was old enough, you got a job. Who looked after him then? I don't suppose you could take him with you.'

'No.' Abby conceded the point. 'To begin with I employed a baby-minder, but when he was old enough I got him into a day nursery. I was lucky. Places in day nurseries are not easy to find.'

'And you didn't write to Oliver? You didn't see him after you left Rothside?'

'Why should I?' began Abby impatiently, and then stopped. Why should she appease his curiosity? He had not shown any interest in her during the past eleven years. Why should she satisfy whatever urge was driving him to ask her these personal questions?

'I think it's time I left,' she declared, finishing her coffee and getting to her feet. 'I—thank you for lunch. It was— very nice. If I don't see Mrs James again, will you tell her——'

'*Abby!*' Piers' tormented voice halted her, and she became aware that he had stopped his pacing and was standing facing her, his hands pushed deep into the pockets of his jacket. 'Abby, you can't go yet.'

She stiffened automatically. 'Why not?'

'Because you can't.' Piers heaved a heavy sigh. 'We haven't finished talking——'

'I have.'

'Abby, we have eleven years to make up.'

'To make up?' Abby shook her head. 'Oh, no, Piers. No, you're wrong.' She held up her head. 'You—you may believe that your involvement with Matt entitles you to his—his confidence, his friendship; and—and you're possibly right. But I—I—you and I, that's a different matter, and just because you're helping Matt it does not give you the right to interrogate me about the way I've lived since I left Rothside.'

'Abby——'

'No, listen to me. Our lives are separate, Piers, separate! I—I don't expect anything from you, and—and you shouldn't expect anything from me.'

Piers' eyes narrowed. 'I could ask Matthew, you know.'

Abby shrugged. 'That's up to you.'

'Don't you care what I might tell him about you?'

'Oh, Piers——' Abby gazed at him tremulously. 'What do you want from me? Why have you brought me here? What do you really hope to achieve?'

'I've told you.' Piers' was abrupt. 'I wanted us to talk, to be civil with one another; if possible, to be friends.'

'Friends!' Abby was incredulous. 'Not a month ago, you said you hoped you never saw me again!'

Piers inclined his head. 'I know.'

'Then——'

'All right,' he moved his shoulders carelessly, 'perhaps I spoke recklessly. Perhaps I didn't mean it.' He paused. 'Perhaps I resented the fact that you could still get under my skin.'

Abby's lips parted, but no words came. She could only stare at him silently, her expression eloquent of her disbelief. 'W—what?' she got out at last. 'What did you say?'

'You heard me.' Piers spoke with some self-derision. 'Yes—pathetic, isn't it? After all this time I discover that I still want you.'

'You're crazy!' Abby made for the door, intent on putting as much space between her and Piers as possible. She didn't stop to examine what his words meant or indeed what they might mean to her. Her only intention was to get away from him, and from the insidious awareness that she was not immune to his disturbing personality. But Piers was there before her, blocking her exit, and when she whirled around to find the other door, his hands on her upper arms prevented her escape.

'Cool down,' he exclaimed roughly, holding her in front of him without making any attempt to draw her back against him. 'All I said was that I still wanted you, Abby. I do. But——' he let her go, 'I have no intention of making the same mistakes again.'

Abby drew a deep breath, fighting back the unexpected sense of anticlimax his words had provoked. For a few moments, she had really believed he had brought her here to make love to her, and although her initial reaction had been to panic, as her pulses subsided she realised her real fear had been of her own response.

Schooling her features, she turned to face him, forcing herself to behave as if his words had not torn her carefully erected defences to shreds. 'You'll take me home now?' she requested, holding his gaze, and knew a helpless resentment when he politely bowed his head.

'If you insist.'

But before he could open the door behind him, a knock came at the panels, and when he turned and called: 'Come in!' Mrs James' apologetic face appeared.

'Sorry to disturb you, sir, but Partridge is here. Apparently there's been some flooding down in the long meadow, and he wants a word, if you've got time.'

'Of course.'

Piers cast an uncertain look in Abby's direction, and she, misinterpreting his hesitation, said at once: 'Couldn't Hedley drive me home? To save you the trouble. I'm sorry I can't walk, but with the rain——'

'That's right, sir. I'll call him, if you like,' agreed Mrs James, apparently eager to get their unexpected visitor off the premises, but Piers waved her suggestion aside.

'I'll take Mrs Roth home after I've spoken to Partridge,' he declared harshly. 'My only concern is that you may have to wait a few minutes,' he added to Abby, and ignoring her indignation, he stalked off across the hall.

'Well now . . .' Mrs James evidently thought it was incumbent upon her to entertain their visitor until her employer got back. 'Would you like some more coffee, Mrs Piers? I'm sure what you've got there is cold, and it's no trouble——'

'Thank you, if I could just use the bathroom again,' Abby declared stiffly, and Mrs James turned obediently to show the way to the stairs.

However, Abby had no intention of being escorted yet again. 'I do know the way, Mrs James,' she informed the housekeeper firmly, as they reached the bottom of the stairs. 'Thank you for your assistance. If you'd just tell Mr Roth where I've gone . . .'

The dismissal was as adept as any Mrs James had experienced before, and with only a faint tightening of her lips to show her disapproval, she walked away. Watching her, Abby knew a moment's compassion, but she and Mrs James had known one another too long for Abby to have any delusions as to where the housekeeper's sympathies lay.

Nevertheless, it was strange walking up the gracefully-curved staircase again, feeling the soft carpet giving beneath her feet, and noticing that although its colour had changed, the elegant oak panelling had not. At the head of the stairs, a wide landing, as big as Aunt Hannah's kitchen at the cottage, gave access to the other first floor rooms, and corridors led off in three directions, all cream and gold paint and soft beige carpet.

Standing on the landing, Abby looked down into the hall below, remembering how overawed she had felt in the beginning. She didn't feel overawed now. She had too many harsh memories to feel any sense of intimidation in this house, but the opportunity to explore was irresistible, and forgetting her original objective, she walked slowly along the corridor until she reached the door that led into Piers' room.

This was not the room they had shared when they first got married. That was next door, a much less austere apartment, that Piers had had made over to her own design. But Piers' room was much as she remembered: dark wood; cream walls, with vivid South American prints to provide splashes of colour, curtains and bedspread in shades of brown and apricot. It was attractive, but subdued, the only signs of his occupation evident in the brushes that occupied the dressing table and the square photograph set on the table beside the bed. It was a photograph of Valerie Langton. Abby recognised the rather haughty features with a twisting of her heart. But unable to resist, she crossed the room, picking it up to examine it more closely.

'It was taken at Badminton. Val was competing,' remarked a cold expressionless voice from the doorway, and Abby's consternation was such that she dropped the photograph. It crashed against the side of the table, the glass shattering as it spilled about her feet, and she turned to face Piers helplessly, shaking her head in useless remorse.

'I'm sorry——' She gestured towards the mess at her feet. 'Please—let me take this and have it repaired. I didn't mean to drop it, but you startled me.'

'What are you doing in here?' he demanded, not answering her. 'Mrs James said you'd asked to use the bathroom. Or was that just an excuse?'

'No, I—I did intend to go to the bathroom, but—well,' she squared her shoulders, 'I was curious, that's all.'

'Curious?' Piers propped his shoulder against the door frame. 'Curious about what?'

He was not making this easy for her, and Abby's tongue made a nervous exploration of her lips. 'Look—let's forget it, shall we?' she appealed. 'I'll take this photograph——' she bent to pick up the frame, and then winced when a shard of glass pierced her finger. 'Damn!' She brushed the offending sliver away. 'I'll get this mended——'

'Put it down,' commanded Piers grimly, and Abby met his malevolent gaze with anxious eyes. 'I said—put it down,' he repeated, straightening away from the door, and she laid it carefully on the bedside table, resenting her unspoken obedience. 'Now,' he went on, 'tell me what you're really doing in my bedroom? What did you expect to find? Some lingering token of yourself, perhaps?'

'No!' Abby was indignant. 'I told you—I was curious, that's all.' She came determinedly round the bed towards him. 'If you'll let me pass, I'll do what I came up to do—repair my make-up.'

'Are you sure you didn't come up to find out what changes Val may have made to your colour scheme?' Piers queried harshly, making no move. 'Why don't you go and see? The door's over there. I'm sure you don't need me to show you the way.'

Abby pursed her lips. 'I'm not interested in what Miss Langton may or may not have done.'

'No?' Plainly, he didn't believe her. 'Not if I tell you she's thrown out your beautiful Aubusson carpet, and that little French escritoire you liked so much?'

Abby steeled herself not to respond to his provocation. 'I really don't want to know this,' she said, tensing herself for flight. 'Now, will you get out of my way, or do you want me to call Mrs James?'

'Would you do that?' Piers moved away from the door. 'All right. Go, if that's what you really want. I'll tell Val you approved of her alterations, shall I?'

'You—you swine!' Abby's mouth worked soundlessly. 'All right, show me how she's rearranged the bedroom, and I'll show you it doesn't mean a thing!'

With lazy strides, Piers passed her, crossing the room to fling open the door into the apartment beyond. Abby followed him reluctantly, painfully aware of how difficult it was going to be to maintain her indifference, and then stopped, aghast, on the threshold. The room—*her room*—was exactly as she had left it. The pink and gold Aubusson carpet still covered the floor, the little French escritoire still stood in the window embrasure, and the creamy silk curtains at the rainwashed windows still matched the velvet coverlet on the enormous four-poster bed.

Abby could only stare in amazement, and Piers' mouth twisted with contempt. 'You didn't really think Val would want to occupy the same bedroom we'd occupied, did you?' he demanded scornfully. 'The apartments my mother has had done over for us are not in this wing at all. I'm only sleeping here until after the wedding.'

Abby fell back a step, the raw abrasion of his voice penetrating her thin veneer of apathy. He had done this deliberately, she realised. He had shown her this room, not to tease her but to torment her, to remind her forcibly of the nights they had shared in that bed, and to taunt her with the knowledge that she would never share that intimacy with him ever again. Had he guessed how she still felt about him? Had he devised this demonstration just to crucify her? But no, she had stepped into a trap of her own making, and he must be vastly amused by her feeble efforts to get free.

She looked at him then, saw the cruelty lurking in his eyes, and made an irrevocable decision. Why should she let him get away with it? Why should she let him have it all his own way? She knew she still attracted him: he had admitted as much. And how sweet it would be to cultivate that attraction and then throw it back in his face. It might hurt her as much as it hurt him, but at least she would have the satisfaction of knowing she had left the game on her own terms.

'Okay.' Piers followed her back into his bedroom and closed the door. 'We can go down now.' He passed her, pausing by the door leading out on to the corridor. 'I'm sure you realise our being here alone together will have created enough gossip without inciting more.'

'Yes.' Abby was thinking fast. She would never have a better opportunity than this one, she thought unsteadily. She could consider its development later, but for the present she had to make him commit himself in some way. 'I——' Her hesitant beginning caused him to turn and look at her as she had intended, 'I'm sorry. A—about the photograph, I mean. I didn't intend to upset you. I was only remembering old times, like you said.'

Piers' dark brows drew together. Evidently he was suspicious of her sudden volte-face. He had expected resentment, recriminations; anger even. He had not anticipated an apology. Not from her.

'I suggest we do as you say and forget it,' he countered crisply. 'Shall we go?'

'In a minute . . .'

'*Abby!*'

'Why not?' She had seated herself on the side of his bed and was resting her hands on the mattress beside her, kneading its springy interior. She sighed reminiscently and looked up at him. 'Do you remember? We used to come up here on wet afternoons like this, and——'

His hands on her upper arms jerked her up off the bed, and his tawny eyes were blazing as they looked down into here. 'What the hell do you think you can do to me?' he snarled, shaking her violently. 'We're leaving—now, do you hear? You were right—it was a mistake to bring you here. I must have been out of my mind.'

Abby smiled up at him, content to have achieved so much with so little effort. But she couldn't resist one last salvo. 'What's the matter, Piers?' she taunted. 'Aren't you as indifferent as you'd like me to believe? Does the feel of my body still do things to you? Or has your mother succeeded in convincing you you're impotent as well as sterile?'

The sound of the bedroom door slamming echoed in Abby's ears as Piers' mouth ground into hers. He must have kicked it shut with his foot, she thought, tasting blood on her tongue as her lips were crushed against her clenched teeth. He would not want any involuntary on-lookers to witness what he was doing, and trepidation at the vulnerability of her own position made her fight to get her mouth free.

'Let go of me, Piers,' she panted, when her sustained resistance to the onslaught of his lips caused him to pause for breath. 'I think we're equal now, don't you? I've proved my point, and you've proved that you do still have feelings——'

'Feelings!' Piers' hand gripped her chin, forcing her face up to his. 'What do you know about my feelings? You almost crippled them eleven years ago.'

'That—that's what you believe,' she choked, trying to prise his fingers from her jaw. 'Piers, for God's sake, let me go. I didn't intend for this to go so far.'

'*You* didn't intend,' he mocked harshly. 'What did you intend, I wonder?' He paused. 'Are you curious enough to find out how good we still are together?'

'No!' Abby was appalled, but Piers' face was very serious.

'Why not? It's what we both want, if we're honest.'

'That's not true——'

'No?' His brows arched. 'But you did want to see this room. You did want to see the bed where we spent many happy hours together.'

'No——'

'What do you mean—no? You did. I found you here, remember? And believe me, after what you just accused me of, I deserve some compensation.'

'I—I didn't accuse you.' Abby licked her lips anxiously. 'Piers, all I said was——'

'I know what you said,' he told her huskily, one hand sliding down her back to compel her trembling limbs against his. 'But as you can doubtless feel, I am not impotent, and God help me, I don't intend to suffer the discomfort that letting you go now would bring.'

'Piers, you don't know what you're saying.' Abby was growing desperate. Her crazy plan had backfired and now it was she who was panicking, she who must not give in to the sensual demands of her own body. 'Look—you'll hate yourself if you do this. You'll despise me——'

'I'll despise myself even more if I don't,' he retorted thickly, his fingers finding the zip at the neck of her dress and propelling it surely downwards. 'Don't fight me, Abby. I won't hurt you. It's not as if this was the first time . . .'

'Piers, you can't——' she whispered brokenly, but already the silky folds of her dress had fallen about her feet.

'I think I must,' he responded, with equal fervour, and his mouth curved sensually as one rose-tipped breast spilled from the lace-edged protection of her slip. 'Oh, Abby,' he groaned, 'I have to do this,' and although she moved her head protestingly from side to side, his mouth found and captured the gasping sweetness of hers.

Abby tried to resist, but the aching caress of his hands on her body sent her senses spinning. When the tantalising intimacy of his tongue explored the quivering contours of her lips, her defences collapsed completely, and the searching invasion that followed left her trembling, weak, and clinging to him.

'Help me,' he muttered, drawing her hands to his body, and blindly her fingers disposed of belts and buttons, separating his shirt from his trousers and pressing herself helplessly against the hair-roughened skin that arrowed down to his navel and beyond. Within seconds he was as naked as she was, and they fell upon the soft coverlet of the bed, their mouths still locked together.

Abby was incapable of coherent thought. Her senses had taken over, and the powerful maleness of Piers' body on hers drove away any needs but those of pleasing him. She could feel the muscles of his legs and thighs, the thrusting pressure against her softness, that made her want to make it easy for him. With the blood running like liquid fire through her veins and her own rising passion eloquent in the hungry urgency of her mouth, she arched herself against him, and felt the sensuous pleasure of his ultimate possession.

'Abby . . .' he gasped, as her limbs enfolded him, and she realised with a catching of her breath that it was almost like a new beginning.

The difference came in the pulsating climax that had Abby's nails raking down the sweat-moist skin of his back. She was no teenager now, no inexperienced girl, without any knowledge of what it was all about. She was a woman, and although she had never realised it until now, her responses were much deeper—her enjoyment that much greater . . .

It took an enormous effort to open her eyes afterwards. She was drowsy, replete; satiated with pleasure, and reluctant to move. Complete realisation of where she was and what she was doing was confined to the awareness of Piers' warm body, close beside hers on the bed, one leg still imprisoning both of hers, his arm resting intimately across her breasts.

Where was she? she mused, gazing sleepily up at the delicate moulding of the ceiling, and that first objective thought brought everything back into horrifying perspective. She was at the Manor, she realised in dismay; she was in Piers' bedroom; and most revolting of all, she had allowed Piers to have sex with her, knowing he despised her and that he had no intention of changing that opinion.

Taking a deep breath, she endeavoured to free herself, and her efforts brought Piers' head up from the pillow beside hers, his lazy eyes dark and slumbrous. For a moment, they just looked at one another, and then Abby's face suffused with colour and she turned her head away from him.

He let her get off the bed, making no attempt to detain her, and Abby gathered her clothes together and made for the bathroom. She could not bear to get dressed in front of him, and her footsteps quickened at the awareness of his eyes on her retreating back.

The long mirrors that partially lined the walls of the bathroom gave back her image in stark detail. In the muted illumination coming through the rainwashed windows, it was impossible to avoid the evidence of bruised bare lips and swollen breasts. There were other marks on her body, marks only a lover could have made, and Abby's lips trembled as she ran water into the basin and tried to erase the smell of him from her skin. But she couldn't. It wasn't something she could wash away, and when she emerged from the bathroom to find him dressed and waiting for her, she knew a helpless resentment that he could look so normal.

'Are you ready?' he asked, only the lingering darkness of those cat-like eyes revealing any emotion, and Abby nodded. 'Good. Then shall we go?' he enquired, without expression, and she preceded him into the corridor on legs that felt decidedly unsteady.

Mrs James met them in the hall below, and Abby, supremely conscious of her appearance, bent her head to avoid the housekeeper's inquisitive gaze. What was she thinking? Abby wondered. What version of this would reach Mrs Roth's ears? And how would the older woman react when she discovered how long they had been alone together?

'Mrs Roth is just leaving,' Piers remarked, swinging open the outer door, and as he did so, the swish of tyres on gravel heralded the arrival of another vehicle. It pulled alongside the Daimler Piers had parked there earlier, and even through the driving rain, Abby could not mistake the face that peered at them through the window.

'Your mother's home earlier than expected,' remarked Mrs James, with evident satisfaction, as Malton appeared to offer his umbrella. 'No doubt the rain's spoiled her outing. She'll be surprised to see you, Mrs Piers.'

Abby's eyes were glittering with angry tears as she turned her gaze up to Piers', and as if taking pity on her, he took the umbrella from Malton's surprised hand, and ushered her out the door and across to the Daimler. 'Get in,' he said, harshly, jerking open the door, and Abby quickly did so, thankful to avoid the inevitable confrontation.

'Piers!'

His mother's summons prevented him from joining her, and he turned back resignedly to seek refuge on the porch.

'What's going on, Piers?' Abby heard Mrs Roth ask, her sallow features dark with indignation as she stared malevolently in the girl's direction.

Abby didn't hear what Piers answered. She simply saw him urge his mother indoors. And then, with a brief word of farewell, he crossed the courtyard again, sliding in beside Abby with economically-controlled efficiency.

The Daimler fired at the first turn of the ignition, and Abby sagged weakly in her seat as the car took her swiftly away from the older woman's influence. Nevertheless, she couldn't believe he had done it for her. He wanted to avoid a scene, too, and because it had suited him, she had been spared his mother's invective.

'I hate you, Piers,' she breathed, when she could summon the effort to speak. 'I—hate—you!'

'That wasn't my interpretation,' he responded flatly, turning the car on to the Rothside road. 'Don't say anything, Abby. No recriminations. It's better that way, believe me. What happened, happened. Neither of us was to blame. Let's call it the end of an era.' He glanced her way. 'Perhaps now we can both start again.'

Abby's jaw quivered. 'I wish—I wish I never had to set eyes on you again——'

'Why? Because I made you see yourself as you really are?'

'What do you mean?'

'Come off it, Abby.' His lips twisted. 'You know what I mean. You wanted me just as much as I wanted you.'

'That's not so.'

'It is so.' Piers drew a deep breath. 'Hell, Abby, if you hadn't been made the way you are, that affair with Tristan Oliver would never have happened.'

'I had no affair with Tristan Oliver,' averred Abby bitterly. 'How many more times do I have to say it? And contrary to your supposition, I—I've never slept with other men.'

Piers gave her a brooding look. 'Since Oliver,' he stated grimly, and she drew an uneven breath.

'You won't even consider it, will you? You won't even entertain the possibility that I might not be lying?'

'I saw you—remember?' Piers muttered savagely. 'I saw the two of you coming out of the barn.'

'So what?' Abby blinked the bitter tears away. 'I never denied that I'd been in the barn with Tristan, or that he'd been showing me the pony he'd bought for Lucy.'

Piers snorted. 'The pony he'd bought for Lucy!' he echoed scornfully. 'And that's why you had straw in your hair, and all over the back of your sweater!'

'I told you—I fell,' Abby protested.

'And I'd have probably gone on believing that if you hadn't got pregnant exactly a month later!'

Abby shook her head wearily. 'Piers, we made love that day, you know we did!'

'We made love every day,' he agreed, his eyes darkening with sudden passion. 'God, Abby, if you knew the torment you put me through you wouldn't question my right to demand retribution! I could have killed you. I wanted to kill you. And when I came to London and saw that baby, looking the image of Tristan Oliver——'

'He didn't!' Abby's voice trembled. 'Piers, he was like me. He was fair like me, and his eyes were green, like mine. You just thought he looked like Tristan. Because he didn't look like you. But he is like you—he is! That's why he's so—so stubborn!'

'So why did you run away? Why didn't you stay in Rothside? If I'd seen him every day, if I'd seen him growing up, mightn't there have been a chance that I might change my mind?'

Abby bent her head. 'You know why. Your mother would have destroyed me. She almost did.' She turned her head to look at his taut face. 'Do you really think, at eighteen, I was strong enough to fight both of you?'

Piers shook his head. 'You took the easy way out.'

'The *easy* way!'

'If you'd really loved me, you wouldn't have left me.'

Abby caught her breath. 'If you'd really loved me, you would have believed me.'

'Abby, I'm sterile! God knows, I didn't want to be. I didn't even know that getting mumps could do that to you, not until Mother suggested I have those tests. But it's there—in black and white. I can't father a child. So how could you get pregnant, unless there was someone else?'

They were approaching the cottage now, and Abby felt an overwhelming sense of weariness. It was hopeless. It was like banging her head against a brick wall. And nothing she could do could change the solid belief Piers had that Matthew was not his son.

When he drew the car to a halt outside the cottage, she would have got out immediately, but he leaned across to detain her. 'Wait,' he said, his warm breath fanning her cheek, 'this—well, what's happened—it won't make any difference to my relationship with the boy, will it?'

Abby shrank back against the seat, painfully aware that his mouth was only inches from hers, and that she had an almost overpowering desire to kiss it. The memory, so recently renewed, of that hard mouth crushing hers made her senses tingle, and her skin prickled helplessly as his intent appraisal continued.

'Abby,' he said, and then again, more harshly: '*Abby*,' and she knew by the way his eyes had narrowed that he was no more immune to this disturbing situation than she was.

'I—no,' she got out huskily. 'No, I—it won't make any difference, so far as Matthew is concerned.'

'Good.' He said the word brusquely, but still he didn't draw back, his detaining arm across her midriff, his sleeve brushing her breasts.

Abby felt as if she couldn't breathe, and Piers' face was paler than it had been only moments before. She knew, almost instinctively, that if he had not been conscious of the cottage windows only a few feet from the car, he would have kissed her, and the knowledge of this dried her mouth and moistened her palms.

'God,' he muttered, still not moving away, 'why do I still want you? Why did you come back into my life, just when I thought it was over?'

'Piers——'

'I know. You hate me and despise me,' he said savagely. 'But believe me, not half as much as I hate and despise myself!'

CHAPTER NINE

IF Aunt Hannah wondered why Abby had not invited Piers into the cottage, she refrained from saying so, and Matthew was too intent on hearing all about the school to be very disappointed at his father's abrupt departure.

'What's it like? Did you see the classrooms? Do they have a football pitch?' he asked in quick succession, and Abby had to try and explain that apart from the headmaster's study, she had seen little of the actual school itself.

'But I think they play rugby, actually,' she confessed, remembering the tall goalposts flanking the playing fields. 'Anyway, you'll see for yourself next week. If you're happy with the arrangements, your father and I will be taking you to look around.'

'Great!' Matthew didn't seem at all put out at learning he was to play rugby, and Abby was relieved that at least his future had not been put in jeopardy by her actions.

Her aunt was a different proposition, however, and that evening, after Matthew was in bed, she asked the questions she had not asked that afternoon. 'But going to the Manor,' she exclaimed, in some exasperation, when Abby tried to justify her acceptance of Piers' invitation. 'I'd have thought you had more sense than to tangle with Mrs Roth again.'

'I—didn't tangle with Mrs Roth,' Abby replied carefully. 'She wasn't there. I—Piers and I had lunch alone. At least, as alone as you can be with servants coming in and out all the time.'

'I see.' Hannah kept her own counsel. 'I thought you were a long time. I assumed, foolishly I now realise, that you'd run into difficulties with Piers' mother.'

'Oh—no. No.' Abby shook her head, glad of the warmth from the fire to disguise her hot cheeks. 'Mrs Roth didn't—return, until we were leaving. I—I didn't even speak to her. It was raining, you see, and—and I was already getting into the car.'

'Hmm.' Hannah sounded suspicious, but she didn't pursue the subject. Instead, she started talking about Matthew, and when he was likely to start at Abbotsford, and it was only later Abby reflected that she was unlikely to have heard the last of it.

The next few days were uneventful. Abby heard, via the village grapevine, that Piers and Valerie Langton had left for Germany, and she suffered agonies at the realisation that he probably slept with Valerie, too. She could not bear to think of him sharing the intimacies they had shared with another woman, and she slept badly that week, tossing and turning in her bed beneath the eaves.

The weather improved, and Matthew offered to dig Aunt Hannah's garden over for her. There were lots of things he could do that Aunt Hannah could not, and Abby knew a sense of pride in his willingness to earn his keep.

For her part, the days dragged, enlivened only when Sean Willis came to call on her aunt. He was unfailingly cheerful, and when, towards the end of that week, he invited her to have dinner with him, she accepted without hesitation.

But to her surprise Hannah was not so enthusiastic. 'Do you think it's wise,' she asked, 'going out with another man, when Matthew has only just discovered who his father is?'

Hearing it put like that, Abby herself had reservations. 'I never thought,' she murmured, her teeth digging into her lower lip. 'I hardly ever accept invitations, but Sean has been so kind—and so friendly——'

'Why shouldn't he be?' demanded Hannah impatiently. 'Abby, haven't I told you? You're an attractive young woman. What man wouldn't be proud to take you out for the evening?'

Abby smiled. 'I'll ask Matt,' she decided, after a moment. 'I'll explain that—just as Piers has—has Miss

Langton, I have to have friends, too.'

Hannah shook her head. 'Well, don't be surprised if he objects,' she declared. 'He's male, isn't he? And the laws for men have always been infinitely more liberal than the laws for women.'

Abby nodded. 'Nevertheless, I have to learn to lead my own life, Aunt Hannah. And—and once Piers marries Miss Langton, I doubt if any of us will see much of him.'

As Aunt Hannah had predicted, Matthew produced a sullen face when Abby told him what she planned to do. 'But what if Dad comes?' he exclaimed. 'He's due back today or tomorrow, isn't he? What if he calls round? What will we tell him?'

'The truth, of course,' replied Abby patiently. 'Matt, your father and I are getting a divorce. You know that. What—what I do with my time is my own affair. It's nothing to do with your father.'

Matt sniffed. 'There's no chance of you two getting back together again, then?'

'No chance.'

He sighed. 'Would you? I mean—if he asked you?'

'No.' Abby was abrupt. 'Matt, this is just a waste of time. Your father and I have nothing in common.'

'You have me!'

'Yes—well,' Abby turned away from his searching gaze, 'I must go and get ready. Dr Willis is coming for me at seven o'clock.'

Abby enjoyed the evening, even though she had not really expected she would after her talk with Matthew. They drove into Alnbury, and had dinner at a small but rather exclusive hotel there, and she relaxed as the evening progressed. Sean was good company, and he kept the conversation going with anecdotes about his life as a medical student, and latterly, the difficulties he had had in gaining the villagers' confidence.

'I was the outsider, you see,' he remarked, pouring more wine into her glass. 'The older people didn't trust me, and the younger ones were seldom sick. Except the children, of course. I eventually made it through the kids.'

Abby smiled. 'I know what you mean. Even living away for only eleven years, I can feel the difference. I suppose they regard me as a stranger, too. And Matt—although he doesn't seem to bother.'

'I've noticed he's been helping your aunt with her garden,' Sean commented. 'He's a strong boy. Is he going to school in Alnbury?'

'No.' Abby hesitated. 'I—Piers has decided it's his responsibility to see that Matt gets a decent education. He's sending him to Abbotsford. It's where he used to go.'

'I see,' Sean nodded. 'Very nice. It's a good school.'

'Yes, so I believe.' Abby shifted a little awkwardly. 'I expect you find the situation a little hard to understand.'

'Not particularly.' Sean shrugged. 'The way I hear it, Roth and you split up a few months after your marriage. I suppose seeing you again reminded him of his responsibilities. Paying maintenance isn't quite the same as a personal involvement.'

'No,' Abby agreed, although she wondered what Sean would say if she told him Piers hadn't paid her a penny for Matthew's upkeep. Still, he had tried, she conceded, and he could hardly be blamed for her refusal.

'Anyway,' he went on now, 'it's better for the boy that he should spend time with both parents. One-parent families are all very well, but they do lack balance.'

'Balance?'

'Of course.' Sean paused. 'You know what I mean. A single parent, of either sex, generally spoils the child or over-disciplines him. You seldom get an equal balance. That's where the two-parent family wins out. Two people rarely agree about everything, and that's good. The child is subjected to a mixture of both treatments, and the outcome is usually favourable.'

'You make it sound ideal.'

'And it isn't. I know.' Sean sighed. 'My wife and I had arguments, too. And I'm certainly not saying that two parents who row all the time are better for the child than one who doesn't. All I'm saying is, a child should *know* both his parents. Then, when he's old enough, he can make his own decisions.'

'Even when one parent hasn't seen their offspring for more than eleven years?'

'Even then.' Sean gave her an apologetic smile. 'A boy, particularly, needs his father. Besides,' he leant across to take her hand, 'it gives you a chance to live a life of your own.'

Abby wondered why this proposition seemed less desirable than it used to do. She had always been proud of her independence, but suddenly all it meant was that she was alone. She still had Matthew, of course, and Hannah depended on her now, but the real core of her depression was Piers, and the certain knowledge that when he married Valerie Langton he would have no further right to involve himself in her affairs.

At breakfast the next morning, Matthew made an effort to be polite about her outing. 'Dad didn't come,' he declared, after she had assured him that she had had a pleasant evening. 'I stayed up until after ten, but no one came. Except Mrs Forrest,' he added, discounting the postmistress, and Abby knew a sudden pang that Piers might not realise how much his son was depending upon him.

The day passed slowly. Already November was approaching, and Abby was not looking forward to the long dark nights, when she would have little to do but regret what was past. Hannah, too, seemed a little under the weather, and Abby was concerned when the old lady agreed to rest during the afternoon. Generally, she napped in her chair beside the fire, but today she did not object when Abby suggested she go upstairs. And when Abby went up later to see how she was, she was alarmed to see how frail the old lady looked, tucked beneath the downy coverlet. Sleep had ironed out some of the lines that etched her weathered features, but it had also closed her lids, and with those sharp eyes hidden, her age seemed so much more pronounced.

Matthew was engrossed in doing a jigsaw puzzle on the kitchen table, and leaving him in charge of the cottage,

Abby put on her coat and crossed the green to the doctor's house. She didn't even know if Sean would be at home, but she took the chance that he might be there.

Mrs Davison opened the door to her ring. Abby recognised Sean's housekeeper after seeing her about the village, and it was evident from the older woman's expression that Mrs Davison recognised her.

'Is—is Dr Willis at home?' Abby asked, pushing her hands deeper into the pockets of her overcoat. It was a warm woollen overcoat, and in London she had needed nothing heavier. But with a chill wind blowing round her ankles, she was beginning to wish she had worn a thicker sweater.

'Yes, he's at home,' Mrs Davison agreed, glancing behind her. 'But he's working, Mrs Roth, and I'm not sure I should disturb him. Is it personal?'

'No. No, it's not.' Abby's chin jutted. 'I've come about my aunt, actually. Miss Caldwell. I'm—worried about her.'

'Oh, well——' Mrs Davison stepped back. 'You'd better come in, I suppose.' She closed the door behind them. 'If you'll wait here, I'll tell Dr Willis.'

Sean was not at all put out by her interruption. 'I'll get my bag,' he remarked, after she had quickly outlined her fears. 'Don't worry, I'm sure it's not necessary.'

Abby nodded, and as they crossed the green she tried to divert her thoughts. 'I don't think your housekeeper likes me,' she commented wryly, her breath misting on the frosty air. 'I hope she doesn't think I'm wasting your time. I felt as though I was taking advantage of our friendship.'

Sean chuckled. 'Mrs Davison is fortifying her position,' he remarked, taking her arm to help her evade an uneven crack in the road. 'She's not stupid. She knows our relationship is the most dangerous competition she's had to face.'

'Sean!'

'Well, it's true. If—and I say *if*—if I were to marry again, her position might be in jeopardy. At least, that's how she sees it.'

Abby shook her head. 'We don't know one another that well.'

'In a village of this size, you should know, the most innocent relationships can be misconstrued.'

Abby glanced swiftly at him. 'You—know?'

'About your supposed affair with the Olivers' son? Yes. Your coming back has resurrected all that old gossip. And because it's known that you and I have been seen together, several people have made it their business to inform me of the facts.'

'Oh, God!' Abby knew an intense feeling of weariness. 'Why can't they let it alone?'

'What? When you've just returned to the village bringing a child you insist is Piers Roth's? Give them a little time, Abby. If they want to gossip, let them.' He paused. 'And I'll tell you one thing . . .'

'What?'

'I've never heard anyone criticise you for what happened. It's the Roths who take the blame. They're the "them" we hear so much about. You are one of "us".'

Abby sighed. 'But that isn't fair.'

'What is, in this life? Leave it be. Roth can take it. It's time his popularity took a tumble. And it will, when he marries the Langton girl.'

'Why?' Abby gazed at him.

'Well, have you met her?'

'Only briefly.'

'Stuck-up bitch!' Sean was laconic. 'Can you see her winning the affection of the people around here? I can't.'

'Well——' Abby was rueful, 'Mrs Roth Senior isn't exactly lovable.'

'No. But in her day, she wasn't expected to be. Things are different now, thank God! And I think Roth realises it. But Miss Langton——' Sean shook his head. 'I think he could do better.'

Sean's reassurance after he had examined Hannah was strengthening. 'She's an old lady, Abby,' he told her gently, facing her in the kitchen, with Matthew looking on. 'You have to expect these setbacks. That's why I wanted her to live at Rosemount; why you're here. But don't worry about her. She's stronger than she looks, and something tells me she's not going to give up the ghost without a good fight.'

After Sean had gone, Matthew put the jigsaw aside and paced restlessly about the kitchen. It was nearly five o'clock, and with the curtains drawn, the night stretched ahead of him, dull and uneventful.

'Why doesn't he come?' he muttered, going to the window for the umpteenth time, and Abby had no need to ask who he meant. His attitude was answer enough.

Piers did not come, however, and when she was in the post office the following morning, Abby inadvertently discovered why. She was examining the paperbacks stacked on a circular frame when she heard two women gossiping by the magazine rack.

'No, they didn't come back,' one of the women was saying confidentially. 'Our Susan says they've gone to Paris to choose the wedding dress, but I said Mr Roth wouldn't do that. I mean, it's unlucky for the groom to see the wedding dress before the actual day, isn't it?'

'So where have they gone?' the other woman pondered. 'You don't think they've eloped, do you?'

'Eloped!' The woman who was Susan's mother sounded impatient. 'No, of course they haven't eloped. He's still married, isn't he? To that niece of Hannah Caldwell's. I know they're getting a divorce, but he couldn't go marrying somebody else before it was all legal, could he?'

'I suppose not.'

'Besides, according to our Susan, that little affair isn't all it should be.'

'What do you mean?'

'I'll tell you later.' Susan's mother sounded very smug. 'Did you know Abby Caldwell was up at the Manor last week? I thought not. Well, as I say, you don't know the whole story.'

The second woman was suitably impressed, but Abby

was numb with humiliation. That Piers and Miss Langton
had decided to extend their holiday to include a trip to
Paris seemed the most likely conclusion, but the confirmation that her affairs were common gossip was degrad-
ing.

She waited until the two women had left the shop before
venturing out from behind the metal bookstand. Then,
seeing that Mrs Forrest was busy with another customer,
she made her own escape without buying anything. The
stamps Aunt Hannah had wanted could wait. Right now,
she needed to explain Piers' absence to Matthew.

But in fact she didn't have to. When she arrived back
at the cottage, it was to find him watching for her, and
when she came down the path, he couldn't wait to open
the door.

'Did you see the car?' he exclaimed, before she had had
time to take off her coat. 'It was a Rolls-Royce. Can you
imagine it? A Rolls-Royce coming to bring me a message!'

'To bring you a message?' Abby was totally at sea.
'Where's Aunt Hannah? I want to tell her I didn't stop to
get her stamps.'

'Oh, she's upstairs, I think.' Matthew was too intent on
conveying his own news to care about Aunt Hannah's
whereabouts. 'Mum, look! I've got a letter—from
Grandmama. Go on, read what it says.'

Abby stared at him and then stared at the letter he was
holding out to her. 'This is from—Mrs Roth?'

'Haven't I just said so? Her chauffeur brought it. In a
Rolls-Royce. An old one,' he added pedantically, 'but a
Rolls-Royce, just the same.'

Abby knew a sense of foreboding out of all proportion
to the circumstances as she took the letter, and after she
had read it, that premonition of impending disaster had
not eased. Mrs Roth wanted Matthew to go to the Manor
for tea that afternoon. But she wanted him to arrive early,
so that he could have his first riding lesson with Jerrold.
And she wanted Abby to accompany him!

'Isn't it great?' Matthew gazed at her excitedly. 'I'm

going to ride Hazel. And you're to come, too.'

Abby shook her head. 'I can't——'

'You can't?' Matthew's exhilaration faded a little. 'Why not?'

'Because I can't.'

'Oh——' Matthew thought he understood, 'you think Dad and Miss Langton might be there. Well, they won't—the chauffeur told me. They're not coming home for a few days. They've been delayed, or something. But that doesn't mean we can't go to tea. It will be nice for you to see Mrs Roth again.'

'It won't.' Abby's nails curled into her palms. 'I'm sorry, Matthew, but I can't go. I—I—it wouldn't be right. Mrs Roth and I don't—get on——'

'You don't get on with many people, do you?' Matthew flared untruthfully. 'You just want to spoil everything. You deliberately took me away from my father, and now, just when I'm getting to know him again, you want to spoil that, too.'

'That's not true!'

'It is true. You said my dad wouldn't want to have anything to do with us, and he has. You said he wasn't interested in me, and he is! I think you'd do anything to stop me from seeing him. You don't care about what's right or wrong. You're just jealous, that's all!'

'Jealous?' Abby was appalled.

'Well, aren't you? You think that if you stay away, I'll have to do the same. Well, I won't. I've told the chauffeur to tell Grandmama to expect me, and he's coming back at two o'clock to take me to the Manor.'

Abby shook her head. It was all so much worse than she had imagined. Now Matthew was beginning to believe that she was trying to keep him away from his father's family. He actually believed she was jealous of the attention they were paying him, and how could she disillusion him without destroying his confidence for ever?

'Matt——'

'You can't stop me,' he muttered, in the tone of voice that indicated that he wasn't entirely sure of himself, and

Abby's heart twisted at the confusion in his face. It was
an impossible situation. If Piers had been there, as he was
before, she would have had no qualms about letting
Matthew go. But to send him to his grandmother alone,
not knowing what lies she might tell him ... Abby drew
an unsteady breath. She simply couldn't do it.

'All right,' she said, regretting the words as soon as
they were uttered, 'we'll go—both of us. But not for tea.
Just long enough for you to ride Hazel, and then home
again. Agreed?'

Matthew pursed his lips. 'All right,' he mumbled, after
a moment. 'I suppose it's better than nothing.'

Aunt Hannah was much less enthusiastic. 'Really,
Abby,' she exclaimed after lunch, when Matthew had
gone up to change, 'aren't you stepping out of the frying
pan into the fire? That woman means you no good, mark
my words. I thought she wouldn't let that little incident
of you lunching at the hall go unmentioned.'

'Aunt Hannah, it's nothing to do with that. It's to do
with Matt——'

'Are you sure?' Her aunt looked sceptical. 'Abby, those
servants at the Manor will have told Mrs Roth everything
that happened that day. I could have told you it was only
a matter of time before she summoned you.'

'She didn't summon me.' Abby felt tired. 'Aunt
Hannah, what could she say about my having lunch at
the Manor? Piers invited me.'

'Hmm.' Hannah frowned. 'It was a long lunch, wasn't
it? As I recall it, it was after three o'clock when you got
back here.'

Abby's face blazed. 'Well——'

'Well—what?' Hannah regarded her with her sharp
eyes. 'Abby—Abby, my dear, I'm not blaming you.
Goodness knows, I know you love the man——'

'Loved, Aunt Hannah, *loved*!'

'—but was it sensible to let him take you to his bed?'

'How do you know he did?'

'I know you, Abby. I know what you were like when
he brought you back here. I guessed something had

happened, but I didn't ask because I didn't want to upset you, any more than you already were.'

'Oh, Aunt Hannah——'

'I'm sorry, Abby, but I know Piers Roth of old, don't I! He never could keep his hands off you. I worried about you then, and I worry about you now.'

'There's no need, Aunt Hannah——'

'What? When he spends his time upsetting you?' Hannah shook her head. 'But I thought you'd have had more sense after what happened before.'

'Yes, well——' Abby moved her shoulders. 'Let's forget it, shall we?'

'Can you?'

Abby bent her head. 'I'll have to, won't I?'

Hannah seethed. 'How could he? How could he? Doesn't he have any shame?'

'Aunt Hannah——'

'No. No, I won't be silenced, Abby. You've always had the worst of it. Didn't I know you were pregnant before you walked down the aisle at St Saviour's!'

'Aunt Hannah, I didn't know that—then.'

'No. But it was no thanks to Piers Roth that it didn't happen sooner, was it?'

Abby put her palms to her cheeks. 'I loved him.'

'I know that. Or do you think I'd have stood by and let you marry him, baby or not?'

'I thought you liked Piers.'

'I did. I do.' Aunt Hannah pursed her lips as if that knowledge didn't please her. 'But I don't want you to get hurt again, Abby; not when I'm to blame for your being here.'

'Oh, don't be silly.' Impulsively, Abby put her arms about the old lady. 'For goodness' sake! I'm a grown woman, Aunt Hannah. I—I knew what I was doing.'

'Did you?'

'Yes. And before you start berating me, let me tell you it was—nothing. Honestly. I've forgotten it already. Now stop worrying about me, and go take a nice rest while we're out.'

Hannah was not entirely satisfied with Abby's assurance, but short of calling her niece a liar, there was little more she could say. Instead, she gave in to her pleas to go and take a rest, and Abby left the cottage feeling as if she had won a major victory. And with such paltry weapons, she thought tiredly. Twelve years ago, it would not have been so easy, particularly when, if Aunt Hannah had looked closely into her eyes, she could have glimpsed the frozen tears that belied her confident words.

CHAPTER TEN

IT was years since Abby had ridden in the back of a Rolls, and Matthew, who had never known such luxury, bounced about excitedly. 'What a pity we don't know anybody,' he declared, staring impatiently through the window. 'Imagine if the kids back home could see me now!'

Abby refrained from pointing out that Rothside was his home now. It was natural that Matthew should still identify with Greenwich, with the people he had known there since he first started school.

Rothside didn't feel much like home to Abby either. The place was not strange to her, and the buildings were familiar, but apart from Aunt Hannah, she felt no sense of identification with village life. Her marriage to Piers had changed all that, she realised, first by removing her to the Manor, and then so quickly becoming a place she wanted to escape from. She still wanted to escape, she thought unhappily. Rothside would always be associated with the most painful experiences of her life, and if—*when*—Aunt Hannah no longer needed her, she would have to think seriously of moving on . . .

'You're not very angry because I made you come here, are you?' Matthew asked in a low voice, as they drove up the curving sweep of gravel to the house. 'I mean—I know you and Grandmama aren't very friendly right now, but you always say it's silly to hold grudges.'

'Don't worry about it,' Abby assured him dryly, gathering her handbag and gloves as the Rolls slowed to a halt in front of the house. 'As your grandmother has invited me, she can hardly throw me out, can she?'

'She wouldn't do that,' exclaimed Matthew sturdily, and then, with touching bravado, he added: 'I wouldn't let her.'

Mrs James met them at the door, her sharp eyes bright and inquisitive. 'Well, well! Back again, Mrs Piers,' she remarked caustically, but Abby knew better than to rise to the bait.

'So nice to see you again, Mrs James,' she responded politely, allowing the housekeeper to take her coat. 'You know my son, Matthew, don't you?'

'Of course I do.' Mrs James allowed the boy a tight smile. 'Hello, Matthew. I hear you've come to have a riding lesson.'

'Yes.' Matthew's tone was absent. He was looking about him, reminding himself of his previous visit, and Abby reflected, with some pride, that he was not intimidated by pretension as she used to be. But then he was Piers' son, she acknowledged rather unwillingly. And blood was thicker.

'If you'll come this way, Mrs Roth is waiting for you in the Japanese drawing room,' Mrs James invited now, and Matthew preceded his mother as they followed Mrs James' straight back.

The Japanese drawing room was predictably Oriental in design. Piers' grandfather had spent some time in the Far East, and it was he who had brought back the exquisitely embroidered carpet and tall lacquered cabinets. The delicate porcelain figurines that filled the cabinets, and the many valuable pieces of ivory and jade owed their presence to Piers' grandmother, who had accompanied her husband on many of his journeys and whose taste in antiquity had been exceptional.

But right now, Abby was paying little attention to the fine appointments of the room. Her memories of this apartment were not all good, and the reason for this was here, seated on a stiff-backed chaise-longue, which enabled her to rest her arthritic knee in comfort.

It was almost twelve years since Abby had seen Mrs Roth, and the older woman had aged considerably. Her once thick dark hair was now much thinner, and liberally streaked with grey, even though the roots gave evidence of a concerted effort to hide the fact. Her face was thin-

ner, and in consequence the skin, which had once been
stretched, now hung in folds about her jawline. She was
still a handsome woman, however, her strong features
gaunt perhaps, but full of character, and without the re-
stricting damage to her knee, she would no doubt be just
as intimidating as Abby remembered.

Her mother-in-law looked first at Matthew, Abby
noticed, the steel-grey eyes, so unlike her son's, appraising
the boy with unexpected fervour. If Abby didn't know
better, she would have said that Mrs Roth saw something
in Matthew that his father couldn't—or wouldn't—see,
and she felt an uneasy premonition of something quite
unacceptable.

'Come here, boy. Don't you have a kiss for your grandmother?' Mrs Roth demanded, after only a fleeting glance
for her daughter-in-law. And after Matthew had obeyed
her, she held on to his hands, surveying him more closely,
and saying with gruff affection: 'I hope you don't expect
to go riding like that!'

Matthew flushed, and looked down at his jacket,
sweater and jeans. 'I don't have anything else,' he said,
and Abby's heart went out to him. It wasn't fair of Mrs
Roth to criticise the way he was dressed.

But apparently her mother-in-law's words were not
intended as criticism. 'I knew you didn't have any riding
clothes,' she declared, her smile appearing briefly. 'That's
why I bought you some in Newcastle. If you go upstairs
with Mrs James, she'll show you where you can change.'

Abby's lips parted, but when Matthew turned a helpless
face in her direction she could not disappoint him. 'Yes,'
she said tautly, 'go and change, Matt. It was kind of your
grandmother to think of it. I'm sure they'll suit you very
well.'

Matthew grinned, and after giving his grandmother a
swift hug, he left the room in search of Mrs James. This,
of course, meant that the moment Abby had dreaded had
come, and her limbs stiffened instinctively when her
mother-in-law's cold eyes were turned on her.

'Won't you sit down, Abigail?' Mrs Roth was the only

person who had ever used Abby's full name, and hearing it, Abby was briefly reminded of the interview she had had with Piers' mother, when the older woman first discovered that her son was in love with his secretary. Abby had been terrified then, awed by the imposing figure Mrs Roth had presented in black jacket and riding breeches, her crop switching impatiently against her booted calf. She was not terrified now. Indeed, as she stood there surveying her old enemy, she wondered why she had ever let Mrs Roth intimidate her. She was just a woman, after all, a rather pitiable woman at the moment, whose desire to control her son's affairs had soured every aspect of her life.

Abby took the armchair opposite her mother-in-law. In spite of the fact that she was still tense, she was beginning to feel more in control of herself, and crossing her legs, she said: 'How are you, Mrs Roth? I was sorry to hear you're suffering from arthritis.'

'It's nothing.' Clearly her mother-in-law did not want her pity. 'A fall,' she added tersely, rubbing an involuntary hand over her knee. 'I'm told that an operation may help, but I have a latent distrust of doctors.'

Abby absorbed this in silence, looking about the room. Sunlight was filtering between long green curtains, giving the room a marine-like radiance, highlighting the intricate marquetry on the doors of the cabinets. So much wealth and beauty was bound to impress Matthew, she thought reluctantly, wondering what Piers' mother really thought of her son. So much affection was not characteristic of the woman she had known, and although she stilled her foolish fears, she could not rid herself of the suspicion that Mrs Roth would not treat Matthew in this way unless she had a motive.

Matthew's reappearance, elegantly attired in well-fitting riding breeches and a tweed jacket, polished boots accentuating the length of his legs, stifled her anxieties. He looked so handsome, she thought, so much a part of his surroundings; and on the heels of this, so much like Piers . . .

'I'm ready, Grandmama.' Matthew came forward for inspection, and Mrs Roth's harsh features broke into a satisfied smile.

'A perfect fit, wouldn't you say, Abigail?' she remarked, including Abby in their conversation, and Abby nodded mutely, as she thrust the unwelcome comparison aside.

'Now, go and find Jerrold,' said Mrs Roth firmly. 'You know the way. Tea is at four o'clock, which should give you plenty of time.'

'Oh, but——' Matthew looked helplessly at his mother, and Abby knew he was remembering what she had said.

'Have a good time, darling,' she told him, silencing her fears, and he charged away happily, content that he had her approval.

When he had gone, the atmosphere was ten times chillier, and Abby had to force herself to remain in her relaxed position. Mrs Roth wasn't finished with her yet, and although she wished she could leave, she resolved not to give in yet again.

'I suppose you miss being able to ride,' she remarked, making a determined gambit. 'You used to enjoy it so much.'

Mrs Roth held up her head. 'I didn't bring you here because I needed sympathy, Abigail,' she declared bleakly, and Abby's lips moved in rueful acknowledgment.

'I don't suppose you did,' she averred, keeping her tone deliberately mild. 'I assume you want to discuss Matt. I suppose you expect me to be grateful that you're giving him this chance.'

'I expect nothing of you, Abigail,' retorted Mrs Roth coldly. 'Except perhaps the morals of a guttersnipe!'

'What do you mean?' But Abby knew what was coming, and prepared herself for it.

'I mean your coming here last week when I was out. I mean the amoral way you behaved, attempting to seduce Piers, so that his petition for desertion would not stand!'

Abby knew a moment's intense anger that Piers' mother should think she still had the right to speak to her in this way, and then relief that it was nothing worse made her suddenly want to laugh. It was so pathetic. She wasn't a child any more, someone Mrs Roth could threaten or intimidate. She was a grown woman, capable of meeting her mother-in-law on equal terms, and if Mrs Roth thought she could get away with bullying her, she was very much mistaken.

'I didn't seduce Piers,' she replied carefully now, maintaining her indolent position. 'And he didn't seduce me.'

'He has more sense——'

'But,' Abby's tone sharpened at the deliberate insult, 'that's not to say we didn't make love. We did.' She ignored the other woman's hoarse intake of breath, enjoying her brief sense of triumph. 'Didn't Mrs James tell you? I was firmly convinced she would.'

'You're lying!'

'Am I?' Abby moved her shoulders carelessly. 'Why don't you ask your housekeeper where we spent the afternoon?'

Mrs Roth's sallow face suffused with unhealthy colour. 'Are you telling me you're going to contest the divorce?'

'I—no.' Abby forced herself to remain calm. 'What—happened—was unpremeditated. It doesn't alter anything. Piers can have his divorce. It was never my intention to blackmail him, if that's what you're implying. But don't imagine you can control my actions any longer, Mrs Roth. You can't. You don't have the power.'

'Oh, don't I?' Mrs Roth's hands were trembling as she lowered her swollen leg to the floor. 'Let me tell you, I'm not as helpless as I appear.'

'I never thought you were.' Abby sighed. 'Mrs Roth, I don't want to argue with you. I didn't ask to come here, and believe me, I'll be as happy as you will when it's time for me to leave. Let's call a truce, shall we? For this afternoon, at least. For Matt's sake, if for no other.'

Mrs Roth's face convulsed. 'You are completely without shame, aren't you?' she cried. 'How dare you think you can sit there and admit to inveigling my son into making love to you, and then imagine I might condone it——'

'I never imagined that.'

'No, but you enjoyed telling me, didn't you? You don't care that because of you my son's life has been ruined!'

'That's an exaggeration.'

'He would have married Melanie Hastings, if it hadn't been for you.'

'He didn't love Melanie Hastings.'

'Love!' Mrs Roth snorted. 'I should have expected something like that from you. How much good did love do you when Piers found you out? Love soon went out the window when reality came in the door.'

Abby bent her head. 'I think all this has been said, Mrs Roth. Isn't it time to let it rest?'

'Rest? Rest?' Mrs Roth was outraged. 'Oh, yes, you'd like that, wouldn't you? You'd like me to overlook your behaviour and go on as if nothing had happened. I knew there'd be trouble, as soon as I heard you'd come back to Rothside. You couldn't wait to start interfering in Piers' life once again.'

'It wasn't like that.' Abby lifted her head. 'Mrs Roth, Matt is Piers' son. Whatever you say——'

'I know.'

Abby's chest felt suddenly tight, as if someone had put an iron band around it and was squeezing hard. 'You know?' she echoed weakly. '*You know . . .*'

Mrs Roth made a pretence of searching for her handkerchief, but Abby had the suspicion that Piers' mother had not intended to blurt it out like that, and was giving herself time to pick her words. 'Yes,' she declared at last, blowing her nose on the handkerchief. 'I—I've known for about three weeks now. Soon after Piers brought Matthew to the house.'

Abby had to grip the arms of her chair very hard to force away the wave of faintness that swept over her at Mrs Roth's words. She was suddenly reminded of the sense of apprehension she had felt upon coming here, and

although she told herself she had nothing to be frightened
of, fear, like a poison, was draining her spirit.

'How—how do you know?' She had to ask, and her
mother-in-law straightened her spine.

'That doesn't matter now,' she averred. 'What does
matter is that because of Matthew you're going to do as I
say.'

Abby's mouth was dry. 'Do as you say, Mrs Roth?
What do you mean?'

'I mean I want you to leave Rothside, Abigail. I want
you to pack up and go back where you came from.'

'Leave? Leave Rothside?'

Abby was finding it incredibly difficult to think at all,
let alone coherently. It had all happened too fast, too
unexpectedly, and she was still too bemused by Mrs
Roth's declaration to do anything but sit there like a
statue. How did Mrs Roth know? How had she found
out? The implications of what it might mean to her and
to Matthew would have to wait. Right now, all she was
doing was reeling from the shock.

'Pull yourself together, girl!'

Mrs Roth's harsh denunciation rang familiarly in her
ears, and instinctively Abby's brain began to clear. It
wasn't the first time Piers' mother had succeeded in re-
ducing her to a stammering idiot, but it was going to be
the last, she told herself furiously. With anger taking the
place of confusion, she found the strength to fight her,
and with carefully contrived self-possession, she said: 'I
have no intention of leaving Rothside, Mrs Roth. You'll
have to think again.'

The silence that followed her words was taut with
menace, but Abby steeled herself not to be afraid. There
was nothing this old woman could do, she told herself
fiercely. She had only to wait and sit it out. Mrs Roth
was powerless.

'You realise, of course, that I can make you change
your mind.'

The words fell like drops of water into a silent pool,
circling and spreading until every inch of space was

engulfed and echoing with their resonance. Her mother-in-law certainly had a gift for timing, thought Abby caustically, but she refused to be drawn into yet another fruitless exchange.

With a determined effort she got to her feet, looking down on the older woman from the advantage of her superior height. 'I don't think this is getting us anywhere, Mrs Roth,' she said firmly. 'I'm pleased that my innocence has been vindicated at last. I'm pleased that you now acknowledge Matt as your grandson. But making threats about my leaving Rothside is simply futile, and we both know it. Don't worry, I'll keep out of Piers' way. I have no intention of making a fool of myself all over again.'

'I didn't say I acknowledged Matthew as my grandson,' Mrs Roth incised quietly, and Abby's half turn was arrested.

'I beg your pardon?'

'You heard me.' Mrs Roth looked up at her coldly. 'I've made no statement to that effect.'

'But you said——'

'I said I knew Matthew was Piers' son. I didn't say I intended to broadcast the fact.'

Abby caught her breath. 'That's splitting hairs. Piers——'

'Piers doesn't know. Nor will he—ever. Not from me.'

'But——' Abby was bewildered, and it was evident from Mrs Roth's face that she had had her revenge.

'You see,' she said, 'I told you I held all the cards. So long as Matthew is vulnerable, you don't have a leg to stand on.'

Abby's fists clenched. 'What do you intend to do?'

'I'll tell you.' But Mrs Roth took her time. 'If you agree to leave Rothside, if you agree to allowing Matthew to stay with us and attend school at Abbotsford, I'll never tell him that he's a bastard——'

'He's not!'

'Will he believe you, do you think?' Mrs Roth waved a languid arm. 'If you deprive him of all of this?'

'You old hag!' Abby's lips trembled.

'Calling me names won't solve anything,' Mrs Roth sneered. 'You and I understand one another, Abigail, and you know I mean what I say.'

'I'll tell Piers what you've said,' exclaimed Abby recklessly. 'I'll tell him you know the truth.'

'He won't believe you.' Mrs Roth was contemptuous. 'He didn't believe you before, so why should he believe you now? And in any case, what you're accusing me of is so unlikely, he'd probably laugh in your face!'

'Unlikely!' Abby almost choked. 'You're an evil woman!'

'I'm a determined woman,' retorted her mother-in-law coldly. 'And I want you out of Piers' life—for good!'

Abby was still standing, as if frozen, when the door behind her opened to admit her son. With his face ruddy from the sharp air, and the glow of vitality and well-being creating an almost tangible aura about him, his expression made a sharp contrast to his mother's pale withdrawn features. And as if sensing the atmosphere in the room, his eyes went first to his mother, but Mrs Roth quickly moved to distract his attention.

'Well,' she challenged, 'how did you get on? I don't see too much mud on your breeches. How many times did you fall off?'

Matthew's smile appeared, but he was not happy, and as if drawn by a magnet, his gaze turned to his mother again. At once, his smile dissolved and his expression grew troubled, and Abby knew an almost overwhelming urge to throw herself on his mercy. But she couldn't do it. It wouldn't be fair. Matthew was only a boy, little more than a child. And she did not doubt that Mrs Roth would use any weapons in her power to destroy their relationship if she could.

'Is something wrong, Mum?'

Matthew's anxious question drew a warning glance from her mother-in-law, but Abby managed to shake her head. 'Of course not,' she denied, schooling her breathing with difficulty. 'Did you have a good time? What did Jerrold say?'

'He said I did very well for a first attempt,' Matthew answered, still looking at her and not his grandmother. 'I only fell off once, and that was because I didn't know how to get astride.'

'So you enjoyed it?'

'Yes.'

'Good,' Abby nodded, wishing he would look anywhere else than at her, and although she knew it was not through any compassion for her that Mrs Roth intervened, she was relieved when the old lady attracted his attention.

'You must come again—and soon,' Mrs Roth declared. 'In fact,' she glanced triumphantly at Abby, 'your mother's been telling me she wouldn't object if you stayed at the Manor sometimes. Would you like that?'

'Stayed at the Manor?' As Abby endeavoured to recover from this sudden attack, Matthew's eyes shifted back to his mother. 'Do you mean we might both come and stay with you and Dad?'

'Your grandmother means you, Matt, not me,' Abby got out tautly. 'You know—well, you know your father and I are getting a divorce. There wouldn't be much point in my being here, would there?'

Matthew caught his lower lip between his teeth. Then he turned back to his grandmother. 'Is that right? You mean just me—on my own?'

'Don't you want to stay at the Manor?' Mrs Roth held out her hands towards him. 'Wouldn't you like to see the nursery where your father used to sleep? I'm sure Mrs James could fix up one of the guest rooms exactly as you'd like it, and in the evenings you and I could play cards together.'

Matthew hunched his shoulders. 'I don't play cards.'

'I would teach you.'

'I like watching television.'

Mrs Roth sighed. 'We have televisions here, too, Matthew. I only meant that you wouldn't be bored. Your father and I—and your stepmother—would see to it that you enjoyed your stay.'

'I'm sure you would . . .' Matthew shrugged a little awkwardly. 'It's just that—well, I want to come and visit again, you know that, and you and Dad have been really kind, but—I couldn't leave Mum. I mean, she has no one else.'

'She has your aunt,' retorted Mrs Roth in a clipped tone. She was not used to being thwarted, and evidently she had expected no opposition from this quarter. 'Matthew, your mother's a young woman. Have you ever thought she might want to lead her own life, free from the restrictions a boy of your age can create, that she might want to get married again?'

Abby opened her mouth to deny this, and then closed it again. With her mother-in-law's eyes upon her, she dared not defend herself. But when her son turned to look at her, with consternation on his face, the need to reassure him got the better of discretion.

'That's not entirely true, Matt,' she stated, ignoring Mrs Roth's expression. 'I've never regarded you as a restriction, and nor do I plan to get married again.'

'But you wouldn't mind if I came to stay at the Manor?'

Abby moistened her lips. 'I—if it's what you want.'

Matthew stared at her, his mouth working. 'You don't want to get rid of me?'

'Get rid of you?' Abby was horrified. 'Of course not!'

'What your mother means is, she wouldn't stand in your way if you decided you liked living at the Manor better than Ivy Cottage,' said his grandmother impatiently. 'Matthew, you're my grandson, your father's son. Don't you realise—when your father and I are dead, Rothside Manor will belong to you!'

Abby wanted to say something then. She wanted to cry that it wasn't fair to weigh the scales so heavily in the Roth's favour, that no boy of Matthew's age should be made to make such an impossible choice. How could a child be expected to weigh the dubious merits of the material benefits the Roths had to offer against loyalty and affection and love?

'Your mother may leave Rothside,' Mrs Roth persisted. 'Without you to worry about, there won't be anything for her to do, and I've no doubt she'll find it much easier to get a job in London than in the north-east of England.'

'But what about Aunt Hannah?' Matthew's fists were clenched. 'Mum, you can't leave Rothside. What would Aunt Hannah do? You know she doesn't want to be put into a home!'

Abby drew a steadying breath. 'I suggest we leave it for the time being,' she declared, meeting her mother-in-law's gaze with taut determination. 'It's not something that can be decided on the spur of the moment.' She turned to her son. 'Matt, go and get changed. We're leaving. You can have tea with your grandmother another day.'

Mrs Roth's lips were pursed. 'There's no need to change, Matthew. The clothes you are wearing are yours. Go and collect your other things, if you like, but keep your riding gear for the next time you come.'

Matthew's hesitation was slight, and after he had gone Abby prepared to face her mother-in-law's anger alone, but in this Mrs Roth was thwarted. 'Shall I ask Susan to serve tea now, madam?' asked Mrs James from the open doorway, and her employer shook her head impatiently, annoyed at the interruption.

'Not now, Mrs James,' she exclaimed, her malevolent gaze fixed on Abby. 'My grandson and his mother are leaving. Ask Porter to bring around the car.'

'Yes, madam.'

Mrs James withdrew with a speculative look at Abby, and as the door closed, Mrs Roth spilled her venom.

'You have forty-eight hours to decide your son's future,' she told the girl chillingly. 'After that, I will wash my hands of him, and I shall see that he knows why!'

As soon as they were in the car, with the glass partition separating them from the chauffeur, Matthew demanded to be told what had happened in his absence.

'Why did Grandmama ask if I wanted to go and stay at the Manor? What had you been saying to her? Whose suggestion was it?'

Abby sighed, resting her head back wearily against the upholstery. 'It was your grandmother's suggestion,' she replied flatly. 'I had nothing to do with it. I—she probably has your best interests at heart. She knows I can't give you the kind of life they can.'

Matthew heaved a breath. 'But I thought it was all agreed. Dad said I was to go to Abbotsford, and I was to live at the cottage with you and Aunt Hannah.'

'I know.'

'So why does he want me to live at the Manor now?' He hunched his shoulders. 'You don't really want to leave Rothside, do you?'

Abby felt a shudder run through her. 'I—I don't know.'

'But you said you didn't mind coming back here. You said you owed Aunt Hannah such a lot, and that it was your duty to help her.'

'I know.'

'So why has Grandmama got the idea that you want to leave? Did you say that to Dad when you saw him?'

'No.' Abby turned her head away from him to stare out of the car window. 'Matt, it isn't as—easy as all that.'

Matthew shook his head. 'I don't understand. What will Aunt Hannah say?'

'We'll have to find out, won't we?' Abby's voice was tight, but she couldn't help it. She was in a blind alley, and Mrs Roth had left her little room for manoeuvre.

Hannah met them at the cottage door, her expression eloquent of the misgivings she had had about the outing. Her sharp appraisal of her niece's features did not go unobserved, and after Matthew had gone upstairs to change, Abby spread her hands in mute submission.

'All right, Mrs Roth did have an ulterior motive for inviting me to the Manor. But I can't talk about it now. Not while Matt's around.'

Hannah sighed. 'What's she been saying now? Surely she doesn't still think she has any influence over your life?'

'Oh, yes,' Abby was bitter, 'she still thinks that all right. And when you hear what she had to say, I think you'll agree that she's right.'

Sean Willis arrived as they were having tea. Hannah looked at him in surprise when Abby let him into the kitchen, and his smile was rueful as he greeted the old lady.

'It's all right,' he said. 'This isn't an official visit. I'm hoping I can persuade Abby to babysit for me for an hour. Mrs Davison is out, and I've just had an emergency call.'

'Of course.' Abby reached immediately for her coat. 'I'll see you later, Aunt Hannah.' She drew her lower lip between her teeth. 'You don't mind, do you?'

'Go along with you.' Hannah started clearing the table. 'Matt can help me with these dishes. Who is it?' She looked at Sean. 'Old Mr Meade from Bank's End?'

'No.' Sean chuckled. 'Actually, it's young Mrs Crossley from Warwick. Her baby's on the way, and the midwife thinks there are complications. Nothing too serious, I don't think. I should be back before eight.'

In fact, it was after ten when Abby heard Sean coming into the house. Miranda had been in bed almost three hours, and Abby had spent the time turning over the problem of what to do about Matthew. The television was on, but she had scarcely looked at it. Her head ached with the effort of trying to find a solution to her problems, and although she knew there seemed no way out, her heart refused to accept it.

Sean came into the sitting room loosening his tie, his tired features mirroring his concern. 'I'm so sorry,' he said. 'It took rather longer than I expected. And as the Crossleys don't have a phone, there was no way I could let you know.'

'Don't worry about it.' Abby got to her feet, hiding her own troubles behind a smile of reassurance. 'Honestly, I don't mind. And Miranda's been as good as gold.'

Sean grinned. 'She's a good kid.'

'What about Mrs Crossley?' Abby arched her brows. 'Is everything all right?'

'Now it is. She had a little girl, too. Unfortunately, she was a breech birth, and they can be the very devil.'

Abby nodded, and then, noticing his worn expression, she exclaimed, 'Look, let me get you a cup of tea before I go. You look exhausted. Sit down. Miranda showed me where everything is, when I prepared her supper.'

'Well, only if you'll join me,' said Sean, sinking down on to the couch Abby had just vacated. 'I could do with some female companionship. Please!'

Abby sighed. 'All right. But it will have to be quick. Aunt Hannah will be wondering where I am.'

'She'll know,' declared Sean comfortably, when the tea was made and Abby was seated beside him. 'Hmm, isn't this cosy? I'd forgotten what it's like to have a pretty woman waiting for my return.'

Abby shook her head, and as she did so, Sean studied her taut expression. Then, almost out of the blue, he said: 'I hear you had tea at the Manor this afternoon. Did Mrs Roth bury the hatchet?'

Abby suppressed a half hysterical sob. 'Yes,' she averred wryly. 'In my head.'

'If you're wondering how I found out, Mrs Crossley's mother is Mrs James' sister. News travels fast in Rothside, as you know.'

'Hmm,' Abby nodded, sipping her tea. 'I suppose it was a newsworthy occasion. Everyone knows there's no love lost between Mrs Roth and me.' Her lips twisted bitterly. 'I wonder what Mrs James said. There's not much goes on at the Manor that she doesn't know about.'

Sean put down his cup and regarded her gravely. 'You sound distressed. I'm sorry if I've upset you. I didn't mean to.'

'It's nothing.' Abby forced a smile. 'I suppose you know all about us. Being a doctor, people confide in you.'

Sean reached across and took her hand. 'That sounded bitter. What is it? What's happened? Why are you so tense all of a sudden? Is it something I've said?'

'Oh, no. No.' Abby shook her head. 'Look, I'd better be going——'

'Not yet.' Sean held on to her hand. 'Abby,' he chose his words with care, 'Abby, if there's anything I can do—you have only to ask.'

'There's nothing anyone can do,' Abby retorted swiftly, withdrawing her fingers. 'Thank you for the tea——'

'Wait!' Sean made no attempt to get up from the couch, even though she was now on her feet. 'Abby, I really would like to help you.' He paused. 'If it makes it any easier for you, I can guess what your problem is. It's Matthew—and the fact that the Roths doubt his identity.'

Abby gasped. 'How do you know that?'

Sean sighed. 'Abby, when you've been a doctor as long as I have, you get to know how people's minds work. It was obvious there would be gossip. You knew that. Particularly after the way you left Rothside.'

Abby's shoulders sagged. 'And what do—*people*—say?'

'Oh, you know. Is he or isn't he? Most people seem to believe he is.'

'They do?' Abby shook her head. 'All except one,' she muttered half inaudibly.

'Piers?' suggested Sean, hearing her, and she flushed. 'Yes.'

'But why?' Sean rose now to face her. 'Oh, I don't mean that old story about Tristan Oliver, I mean why should he doubt it? Surely the odds were definitely in his favour, whatever your relationship was.'

Abby bent her head. 'If I tell you, will you promise not to tell anyone else?'

'You have my word.'

Abby sighed. 'Piers had a medical examination before our marriage. He—he was told he was sterile.'

'Sterile!' Instead of sympathising, Sean looked amazed. 'But it's patently not true, is it?'

Abby swallowed. 'Isn't it?'

'Hell, you know it isn't.' Sean pushed impatient fingers through his already unruly hair. 'Abby, I'd stake my life on the fact that Matthew is Piers' son. Good God, the evidence is unmistakable!'

Abby's nerves clamoured. 'You think so?'

'Dammit, I'd swear it. Don't you think they're alike?'

'Well, yes, but——'

'But what?' Sean's eyes narrowed. 'Is there any doubt?'

Abby's head came up. 'Of course not.'

'Well then——'

'Sean, Piers won't believe me. He's seen the report Dr Morrison compiled.'

'Morrison!' Sean's mouth turned down. 'You mean, Morrison arranged the examination?'

'Of course.'

Sean shook his head. 'Well, I have to say, Dr Morrison's retirement was long overdue.'

'You mean—he made mistakes?' Abby's spirits stirred.

Sean nodded. 'Oh, nothing I'm prepared to accuse him of, but there are one or two people in this village who are lucky to be still alive.' He spread his hands. 'He was old. And he was suffering from rheumatism. He simply didn't have the patience.' He grimaced. 'Almost an apt pun.' He paused. 'But why should Roth have had this examination? He looks perfectly healthy to me.'

Abby hesitated. 'It was his mother's idea. He—he had mumps when he was eighteen. It was she who suggested he see Dr Morrison.'

Sean made a sound of irritation. 'But Abby, thousands of men suffer from mumps without it causing them any side-effects whatsoever.'

'I know. But I didn't know anything about it. Until—until——'

'—you found you were pregnant,' Sean finished for her, and she nodded. 'Poor Abby! So that's why you ran away. And now you're back, it's all starting over.' He frowned. 'But tell me, if Mrs Roth doesn't believe Matthew is her grandson, why is she making such a fuss of him? From what I hear, she's becoming very fond of him.'

'She is.' Abby closed her eyes for a moment as the prick of tears became almost too much for her. 'Oh, she knows

Matt is Piers' son. Or at least she says she does. But she's never liked me, or approved of me, and—well, she wants to take Matthew away from me.'

Sean was appalled. 'She can't do that!'

'No. Not legally, anyway. But she's threatened to tell Matt that Piers is not his father, and—and if she does, I don't know what he'll do.'

'She's a monster!' Sean gazed at her compassionately. 'Is that why she summoned you to the Manor? To deliver her ultimatum?'

Abby nodded again. 'I just don't know what I'm going to do.'

Sean put his hands on her shoulders. 'You've got to fight her, Abby. You can't let her take Matthew away from you.' He snorted. 'What kind of a man is Piers Roth anyway, that he'd let his mother do his dirty work?'

'Piers may not know.' Abby tried to be charitable. 'He—he's away——'

'In Germany—I know. The Langtons told me. Mrs Langton was feeling unwell earlier in the week, and I was called out to the farm.' He expelled his breath heavily. 'But I can't believe Mrs Roth would do this without her son's approval.'

Abby had come to that conclusion, too, and it didn't help to have it confirmed. 'I'd better go,' she said unsteadily, but Sean wasn't quite finished.

'I've got an idea,' he said. 'When I moved in here, I inherited all Dr Morrison's medical records. You know what I mean. I've got the files on all his patients, both past and present. If I'm lucky, I may still have that report he had prepared. It may take some time, but I'll look if you want me to.'

Abby's lips parted. 'Would you?'

'When you look at me like that, I'd do almost anything.' Sean grimaced. 'Even if it isn't entirely ethical, you are his wife, and these are unusual circumstances. Will you wait?'

Abby glanced at her watch. It was almost eleven, and

he was tired. It wasn't fair to expect him to go looking through medical records tonight.

'Tomorrow,' she said. 'I'll come back tomorrow. It can wait one more day. After waiting all these years for the truth to come out, one more day isn't going to make that much difference.'

Sean grinned. 'If you're sure.'

'You've been marvellous,' she told him huskily. 'Thanks for listening.'

'Any time,' he averred, accompanying her to the door, and watching her intently until she reached the gate of Ivy Cottage.

CHAPTER ELEVEN

SOMEWHAT to Abby's relief, Aunt Hannah had gone to bed by the time she got back. The old lady had evidently waited up for her until after ten o'clock, and the cup of hot chocolate she had prepared for her niece was still warm. But when Abby put her head round her aunt's bedroom door, it was to discover Hannah had fallen asleep, the book she had been reading sliding unheeded from her unresisting fingers. Quietly, so as not to disturb her, Abby removed the book and then turned out the lamp before retiring to her own room.

But sleep for Abby was elusive. Even though she was tired, the conversation she had had with Mrs Roth, Matthew's confusion, Sean's encouragement, her own uncertainty, all served to keep her brain active long after her light was out. She tossed and turned restlessly, trying not to think about Piers, or about the fact that he must be a party to his mother's ultimatum, and fell asleep eventually, to dream about him making love to Valerie Langton in the bedroom Abby and he had shared ...

She overslept the next morning, and came downstairs still in her dressing gown, expecting to find Aunt Hannah and Matthew had already had breakfast. But no one was about, and a little disturbed, she made her way back upstairs.

Checking first on Aunt Hannah, she discovered the old lady was awake but evidently listless, and after taking her pulse, Abby regarded her anxiously. 'How do you feel?' she asked, when Hannah made some impatient comment about her concern. 'I suggest you stay where you are for the time being. There's nothing spoiling.'

'But it's nearly nine o'clock,' exclaimed Hannah fretfully. 'Why didn't you wake me sooner?'

'Because I wasn't up sooner,' replied Abby mildly. 'Just

relax and take it easy. I'm going to make some tea.'

'You were back very late last night, weren't you?' Hannah spoke half reprovingly. 'I thought you and I were going to have a little chat. I didn't know you were going to make a night of it. I think Matthew was upset, too.'

'Matt?' Abby frowned. 'Why?'

'Well, you know how he feels about you and Piers. He doesn't like you going out with other men.'

'I wasn't *out* with another man,' Abby protested. 'Didn't you explain? Baby-sitting is not the same as making a date.'

'I think he thought you were taking too long to be just baby-sitting,' remarked Hannah, and Abby had the distinct suspicion that this had been her aunt's interpretation, too.

'Well, I wasn't,' she said now. 'Sean was late back— Mrs Crossley had a breech birth, and he was exhausted when he got home.'

'Hmm, well . . .' Hannah was grudging. 'You still haven't told me what happened at the Manor.'

'I will.' Abby moved towards the door. 'But I'll make the tea first. I could do with a cup myself.'

Before going downstairs again, Abby made her way to the tiny room Matthew was occupying. It was unusual that all of them should sleep in this morning. She hoped he wasn't sulking about her baby-sitting for Sean.

She opened his door carefully, just in case he was still asleep, and then frowned. Matthew's bed was empty. He had slept in it; the sheets and blankets were tumbled. But it was empty now, and remembering the deserted kitchen, Abby knew an instinctive fear. Where was he? Why hadn't he awakened her? And more practically, why hadn't he had any breakfast? He usually had such a healthy appetite.

Unwilling to disturb Aunt Hannah with her anxieties, Abby hastened downstairs again, wondering if she might have missed him. Matthew could have been outside, in the garden, or even in the parlour. It was not impossible. But it was inconceivable, and after a thorough search she was forced to the conclusion that Matthew had got up and gone out without telling her and without any nourishment. The back door was unlocked, a sure sign that someone had gone out that way, and when she checked in the hall, she found his navy blue parka had gone as well.

It was so unlike him to do such a thing that Abby couldn't help the sense of unease that gripped her. As she filled the kettle, she couldn't help remembering the conversation they had had the previous afternoon, and recalling his troubled questions about their relationship. Surely he had not interpreted her unwillingness to discuss the matter as proof that she wanted him to live with his father and grandmother. Surely they knew one another too well for him to imagine she had any part in his grandmother's invitation. Or had he become upset over her friendship with Sean as Aunt Hannah had intimated. The idea that he might have associated the two things together didn't bear thinking about, and she didn't know what she was going to say to Aunt Hannah when she went back upstairs.

By the time the kettle had boiled, she was taut with apprehension. Where could Matthew have gone? Only one place seemed to make any sense, and she wished she had been dressed so that she could have gone out and used the telephone callbox in the village to ring the Manor. At least, whatever the outcome, she would have known the worst. As it was, she had no choice but to pretend that all was well.

It was tortuous, sitting drinking tea with Aunt Hannah, her mind chaotic with the turmoil of not knowing where Matthew was. If only she had not overslept, she might have been able to talk to him. The trouble was, she had let him think she was not averse to the Roths' plans for him, and in so doing she could have lost him for good.

The thought of this was so traumatic, she could not suppress the sob that rose to her throat, and Hannah, misinterpreting its cause, leaned across to pat her sleeve.

'I shouldn't let anything Claudia Roth said upset you,' she declared comfortingly. 'Matthew's a sensible boy. He may be a bit overawed with his own importance right now, but once Mrs Roth finds another diversion, you'll find Matthew's nose will be put out of joint.'

If only that was all she had to worry about, thought Abby bitterly, unwilling to add to Aunt Hannah's concern. Now was not the time to broach the question of what Matthew was going to do. First of all, she had to find him. Then she would get the answer for herself.

Because her aunt was tired, her brain was not quite as alert as it might have been, and Abby was relieved not to have to answer any more searching questions. Later, she might be brought to task for not telling Aunt Hannah the truth, but just now the old lady was content to relax on her pillows and doze for a while.

'I don't want anything to eat,' she said, when Abby suggested she might like some toast. 'Just a little sleep, that's all I need. You go and get Matthew's breakfast. He's a growing boy. He needs it.'

After a swift wash, Abby dressed in purple jeans and a matching shirt, and then, grabbing her warm coat, she left the cottage. It was already half past nine, and her heart hammered unsteadily as she speculated about how long Matthew had been gone. If he had gone to the Manor, he could have left any time after it got light, but if he had run away . . .

Her brain stopped working at this point, and returning the postmistress's greeting with a polite smile, she swung open the door of the callbox and nudged inside.

Malton answered the phone at the Manor, and Abby's mouth was dry as she asked whether her son was there.

'Matthew, Mrs Piers?' the butler enquired in surprise. 'Why should you think that? I was not aware that Matthew had been invited to stay the night.'

'He wasn't. He didn't. Oh—it doesn't matter.' Abby came out of the callbox feeling worse than ever. Matthew had gone. He had run away. And apart from Mrs Roth, there was no one she could turn to.

And then she thought of Sean. Why hadn't she thought of him before? He would help her. He had helped her already. And at least he knew the truth about Matthew.

Mrs Davison answered the door to her knock and regarded her with her usual suspicion. 'Dr Willis is taking surgery,' she declared, blocking Abby's path. 'If you'd like to leave a message, I'll tell him to get in touch with you later in the morning.'

Abby's shoulders sagged. 'It is rather urgent.'

'So is surgery, Mrs Roth.' Mrs Davison was not budging this time. 'As I say, as soon as he's free, I'll tell him you called.'

'Oh—very well.' Abby turned away.

'Is there no message?'

Abby glanced back. 'No, no message. Just that I called, as you said.'

Trudging back across the green, Abby knew an overwhelming sense of weakness. She was not, and had never been, a helpless female, but right now she felt as near to complete vulnerability as it was possible to be. What should she do? What *could* she do? And how could Matthew do this to her without giving her a chance to say a word in her own defence?

She had reached the cottage gate when a vehicle screeched to a halt beside her, and she turned her head automatically, apprehensive of who it might be. She recognised the station wagon at once, and with widening eyes she saw Piers behind the wheel. But it was the sight of Matthew sitting beside his father that made her stop and confront them, her spine stiffening instinctively at the prospect of the battle to come.

Matthew thrust open his door and got out at once, his face red and defensive as he faced her across the grass that edged the kerb. 'Sorry, Mum,' he muttered, his hands pushed deep into his pockets, and Abby moved her shoulders helplessly, not knowing what to respond.

'Go along indoors, Matthew,' his father ordered presently, getting out of the car. 'I'll speak to you later. Right now, I have things to say to your mother.'

'Oh, but——' began Matthew, his eyes darting from one to the other of them. 'I mean—you will tell her why

I did it, won't you? I didn't mean to worry her.'

'That's all right.'

Piers was abrupt, his dark face drawn and impatient as he waited for his son to leave them, but Abby had to intervene. 'Where have you been, Matt?' she cried, wanting to put her arms around him, but Matthew only shrugged his shoulders, keeping his head averted.

'Dad'll tell you,' he said, taking one hand out of his pocket to push open the gate. 'Can I make myself a sandwich? I haven't had anything to eat, and I'm starving.'

Abby shook her head. 'Oh, if you like,' she exclaimed, not understanding any of this, and then she looked at Piers again, steeling herself against his irresistible attraction.

'Shall we get in the car?' he suggested, but Abby only shook her head again.

'Anything—anything you have to say to me can be said here, where everyone can see us,' she declared bitterly. 'I shouldn't like your mother to hear any more gossip, particularly after what she said.'

Piers drew a deep breath. 'I don't care what people say.'

'No, but I have to,' retorted Abby tautly. 'Oh, please— can't we just get on with it, whatever it is? I'm freezing!'

Piers' mouth compressed. 'Matthew was on his way to the Manor.'

'I'd gathered that.' Abby broke off. 'On his way? Didn't he get there?'

'No. I picked him up on my way here,' replied Piers flatly. 'We've been talking for the past half hour. I know I should have brought him back sooner, but it was necessary that he understand the situation.'

'The situation?' Abby's mind felt blank. 'What situation? Yours and Miss Langton's? I think he knows about that. You've made it blatantly——'

'Not about me and Val,' Piers overrode her harshly. '*The* situation; his situation; the reason why I've played such a small part in his life to date.'

Abby gasped, grasping the gatepost for support. 'You—

you mean you've told him about—about——'

'—my believing I was sterile, yes.' Piers put a hand on her arm, but when she flinched away from him, he withdrew it at once. 'Abby, he had to be told. It was better I should tell him. Poor kid, he has every reason to hate my guts!'

Abby was trembling so badly she could hardly stand, but the words of recrimination spilled from her tongue. 'You did it,' she cried, her voice breaking on a sob. 'You did it. You told him. Your mother said I had forty-eight hours! Forty-eight hours! Oh, God—I could kill you, I could kill you! How could you? How could you?'

She had turned to him now, battering his chest with her fists as pain and frustration and humiliation all took a hold on her. 'You Roths,' she sobbed, tears spurting from her eyes, 'you think you own the earth! Oh, God—oh, Matthew! Why was I ever born!'

Piers allowed her to go on for perhaps half a minute, and then, with a muffled oath, he took both arms and imprisoning them beside her body, he marched her to the station wagon. 'Get in,' he said between his teeth, and when she would have argued, he exerted a painful pressure. 'Go on, get inside. Or do you want half Rothside to witness me administering corporal punishment?'

'I won't!' Abby struggled, fighting to get away from him, and then, with a little gasp, the strength went out of her, and Piers forced her into the seat and slammed the door behind her.

She supposed she could have got out while he was circling the car, but he would have only come after her again, and she really was too tired to go on fighting. What did it matter now anyway? Matthew had been told the truth. Mrs Roth had done her worst, and all she could do was hope he would forgive her.

'Now . . .' Piers made no attempt to drive away. He merely turned in his seat towards her, his jaw hard and unyielding. 'Will you tell me what the hell all that nonsense was about, or do I take you back to the Manor and get the truth from my mother?'

Abby slumped. 'Don't pretend you don't know,' she muttered in a lacklustre voice. 'You knew what she was doing. It was probably your idea.'

Piers' arm was along the back of her seat, and hard fingers gripping her nape brought her face round to his. 'What are you talking about?' he demanded, his tawny eyes smouldering. 'I warn you, Abby, I'm losing patience. What the hell has been going on?'

Abby stared at him, but unable to read anything in those glittering orbs, she shook her head. 'You know,' she insisted. 'Your mother made the situation very clear. You've apparently decided that Matthew is your son, after all, and now you want me to bow out of the proceedings.'

'*What?*' If Abby had not been so drained, she would probably have recognised the genuine astonishment in Piers' eyes. As it was, she merely hunched her head deeper into her shoulders, dislodging his bruising fingers, and sinking into despair.

'She told me I had forty-eight hours,' she moaned, turning her head from side to side. 'But now it's too late. It's over. Matthew probably blames me for everything.'

Piers lost his temper. 'For God's sake, did he look as if he blamed you?' he demanded savagely. 'I brought him back because this is where he belongs, with his mother. He knows that, and damn it, I've never disputed it.'

'You've never disputed it because you don't believe—you *didn't* believe—he was your son,' Abby rallied bravely.

'All right—fair comment. But I've got no intention of taking him away from you. And even if I had, Matthew wouldn't go!'

Abby shuffled up in the seat. 'What do you mean?'

Piers drew a weary breath. 'Why do you think he was going to the Manor this morning?'

Abby shrugged. 'I'm not sure.'

'Didn't you know it was because he wanted to let his grandmother know that although he enjoys visiting the Manor, he didn't want to live there?'

'No!' Abby felt a surge of hope. 'You mean—he wants to stay with me?'

'Haven't I just said so?' Piers made a helpless gesture. 'Abby, I don't know what my mother said to you—to either of you—but I do know Matthew knows exactly what he wants.'

Abby swallowed convulsively, looking at him properly for the first time. 'I thought you were in Paris.'

'Me?' Piers shook his head. 'I told you, I was going to Germany. I got home late last night.'

'But—I heard——'

'What did you hear?'

'Well, that—that Miss Langton was supposed to be in Paris, buying her trousseau.'

'Val is in Paris. But I didn't go with her.'

'Oh!' Abby nodded. Of course, Miss Langton wouldn't want Piers to see what clothes she bought for her trousseau.

'So——' Piers regarded her steadily, 'are you going to tell me what my mother said, or do you still believe I know?'

Abby pressed her lips together. 'If—if you didn't know what your mother was doing, why did you tell Matt about—about Tristan?'

'About Tristan?' Piers stared at her. 'What does Tristan Oliver have to do with any of this?' He shook his head. 'Abby, what are you saying?'

Abby blinked. 'What did you tell Matthew then? That—that you didn't know who his father was? Or didn't he ask that question? Was he too stunned to listen to anything after you told him what you believed?'

Piers groaned. 'Did he look stunned when you saw him?' he demanded. 'Abby, get that crazy notion out of your head! I told him I was to blame for our splitting up. I told him how it happened, and how I was almost out of my mind with jealousy. I think he believed me. I think he almost felt sorry for me. He doesn't blame you. If he blames anyone, it will be me, but I'm hoping to spend the rest of my life making it up to him.'

Abby quivered. 'Making what up to him?'

'The fact that I wasted all those years we were apart. The fact that if I hadn't been so bloody proud, I'd have found myself another doctor and got a second opinion.'

Abby couldn't take this in. 'You mean—you mean—you believe that—that Matthew is your son?'

'Haven't I just said so?' Piers' mouth twisted. 'Dear God, Abby, how am I ever going to be able to make you forgive me, when you won't even listen to what I'm trying to say?'

Abby put out a hand, as if to ward him off. 'I—I don't believe you——'

'For God's sake——'

'This—this is another of your mother's ploys to get me to—to commit myself——'

'Stop it!' With controlled violence, Piers thrust her trembling hand aside, and taking her half hysterical face between his hands, he forced her to look at him. 'Abby, I mean what I say. I saw a doctor in London the day before yesterday. The tests were positive. I'm not—I never have been—sterile!'

Abby stared at him, compelled to believe the sincerity of his words. 'But—but why? Why would you do that? Because you're going to get married again? Because Miss Langton needed that confirmation?'

'Val!' Piers expelled his breath heavily. 'Whether or not I was sterile would mean little to Val. Having children is not something she would worry about. So long as she has plenty of money for her horses, she'll be content.'

'Then—you did it for Matt——'

Piers' hands crushed her cold cheeks. 'No.'

'So—why?'

'I did it for you,' Piers told her violently. 'For *us*! Since leaving here, I haven't been able to get you out of my mind, and I knew I had to do something or quietly go insane!'

Abby gulped. 'You don't mean that.'

'Of course I mean it!'

'You're going to marry Valerie Langton. I won't—you can't expect me to—to be used——'

'I am not going to marry Val,' Piers interrupted her harshly. 'If you'd given me a chance to explain I'd have told you that straight away.'

'Not—going to marry Miss Langton——' Abby stammered bewilderedly, and Piers closed his eyes against the unconscious appeal of hers.

'No,' he muttered thickly. 'Why do you think she's in Paris while I'm here? I broke it to her while we were in Wenheim. I knew I couldn't go through with it. Not after what happened between us at the Manor.'

Abby shook her head bewilderdly. 'But—you said you hated me, you despised me——'

'No, you said that,' Piers corrected her huskily. 'I said I hated and despised myself. I did. Because in spite of everything I thought you'd done, I still wanted you—I still loved you.'

Abby quivered, and only now did her own hands leave her lap to grope weakly for his waistcoat. 'You—love—me?'

'Didn't I always?' he demanded, his mouth grim yet sensual. 'God, it took me eleven years to even think I'd got over you. And then you came back, and I knew I never would.'

Abby's quivering fingers drew his hands away from her face and pressed them back against him. 'You—you've told your mother this?' she asked tremulously.

'She knows I'm not going to marry Val. I rang her before I left Wenheim.'

Before he left Wenheim! Abby was beginning to understand.

'Does she know why?' she breathed, holding tightly to his fingers.

'She knows how I feel about you.' Piers looked at her with devastating frankness. 'How could she not? I haven't exactly been able to hide my feelings.'

Abby drew a steadying breath. 'And what did she say?'

'Does it matter?'

'I—I'd like to know.'

'All right.' Piers moved his shoulders carelessly. 'She

said I was wasting my time. That you'd told her you wanted to leave Rothside.'

'What!' Abby was appalled. 'Did you believe her?'

'Does it look as if I did?' Piers used her hands to pull her against him. 'Abby, I know my mother of old. She'd do anything she could to keep us apart.' He paused. 'I suppose that's what all this is about, isn't it? Matthew told me you went with him to the Manor yesterday. What did my mother say to upset you so much? And why should you be so concerned about Matthew's learning the truth? I thought you'd be glad.'

Abby shivered. 'I am—now.' She shook her head. 'Oh, it doesn't matter. Let's forget it. I want to know what Matt said.'

'Later.' Piers' hands slid over her shoulders. 'First tell me what happened yesterday afternoon. I mean to know.'

Abby closed her eyes. 'How can I?'

'How can't you?' he countered, shaking her eyes open again. 'Abby, we must have no secrets. Not now—not ever again.'

Abby bent her head. 'You're presuming a lot.'

'Am I?' Piers' eyes darkened. 'Are you going to tell me you won't forgive me? I wouldn't blame you if you did. But don't tell me you don't love me, because *that* I won't believe!'

Abby shook her head. 'What are you saying?'

'You know what I'm saying. I'm saying we should forget about the divorce, I'm saying we belong together.'

Abby's breathing quickened. 'Your mother will never agree——'

'My mother isn't involved,' retorted Piers grimly. 'Believe me, she's interfered in my life for the last time. Now, are you going to tell me what she said, or do I have to ask her?'

Abby bit her lip. 'She—oh, she said that—that unless I got out of Matt's life for good, she'd tell him he was a bastard.' She stole a glance at his stunned features, and then went on: 'She—she wanted me to leave Rothside. She said Matt could go and stay at the Manor with—with you and his new stepmother——'

'My God!' Piers' angry oath halted her stumbling explanation. 'And she already knew I had no intention of marrying Val. I'd spoken to her the day before. Lord, no wonder Matthew was so concerned! He was afraid you might let his grandmother persuade you, and no way did he want to come and live at the Manor with me and Val.'

'Oh, Piers!'

Abby's eyes mirrored her consternation and Piers was not proof against those tear-drenched green pools. With a muffled exclamation he pulled her closer and bent his head to kiss the vulnerable skin beside her ear.

But Abby's hands pressed against his shoulders. 'Not here, Piers,' she breathed, fighting the urge to turn her lips against his neck. 'I—anyone might see us.'

'So what?' His lips moved against her cheek. 'I can't go on being near you without touching you. God, Abby, I want you so much. You can't deny me this . . .'

His mouth touched hers lightly at first, and then with increasing passion. Ignoring the fact that they were parked in full view of the cottage and its neighbours, he gathered her completely into his arms, opening his jacket and her coat to press her even closer. His mouth opened hers, demonstrating exactly how much he needed her, and Abby's inhibitions dissolved beneath the need to prove her love.

When at last he lifted his head, they were both panting and breathless, and Piers' face was pale in spite of his dark skin. 'I don't want to let you go,' he muttered, 'but I must. There are things I have to do, people I have to speak to. Do you think you can cope with Matthew, until I can get back?'

Abby slipped her arms around his neck. 'You will come back?' she whispered huskily, and he made a wry grimace.

'Try and keep me away,' he told her forcefully, and Abby bestowed another lingering kiss upon his mouth before reaching for the door handle.

'I love you,' she said, when she was outside and Piers had wound down the window to say goodbye.

'And I love you,' he answered, looking at her mouth, so that when she turned away, she felt as if he had kissed her again.

CHAPTER TWELVE

MATTHEW was in the kitchen, munching a cheese sandwich, when Abby entered the cottage. But his face was flushed, as if he had been hurrying, and noticing the telltale trail of crumbs on the rug, Abby give him a questioning look.

'You haven't been in the parlour, have you?' she asked, her own cheeks deepening with colour at the implied connotation, and her son shrugged offhandedly.

'What if I have?' he declared, evidently prepared to bluff it out, and unable to keep her excitement to herself a moment longer, Abby enfolded him in her arms.

'Oh, darling—your father and I are not going to get a divorce,' she exclaimed, after Matthew had made a rather embarrassed withdrawal. 'We're going to live together again. We're going to be a proper family!'

In spite of his attempt to treat the matter casually Matthew could not hide his delight at her words. 'Really?' he exclaimed. 'You really are going to live together? Where? Here? Or at the Manor?'

Abby felt a momentary disquiet. 'Well, at the Manor, I suppose,' she said unhappily, dreading the prospect of having to share a roof with the woman who had done her best to ruin her life. 'I—the details aren't worked out yet, Matt. But the main thing is, we're all going to be together.'

'You're happy?'

'Can't you tell?' Abby smiled.

Matthew bent his head. 'I did see you, you know. You and Dad, I mean. I was looking out of the window.'

'I guessed you were,' said Abby dryly. And then: 'But you did give me a scare when you disappeared. I didn't know what to think.'

Matthew sighed. 'I thought I might get there and back

before you missed me. But it was farther than I thought, and Dad met me on the road coming here, and—well, I expect you know the rest.'

'Not all of it.' Abby frowned. 'Why were you going to see your grandmother? What did you hope to achieve?'

Matthew slumped into a chair. 'It seems pretty silly now. I thought—well, I thought if I told her—myself, I mean—that I didn't want to live at the Manor with them, she might stop encouraging you to go away.'

Encouraging! Abby's mouth was dry. Thank goodness, Matthew need never know the half of it.

'I guess living with Dad would have been okay,' Matthew went on consideringly, 'if it had only been him. I'd have missed you—a lot—but at least I'd have had him. But I didn't want to live with Grandmama and that snobby Miss Langton. It wouldn't have seemed right. And I knew she wouldn't want me around, after they were married.'

'Oh, Matt!' Abby came to run her fingers over his hair and this time he didn't pull away. 'Matt, I thought you'd jump at the chance of living at the Manor. Mrs Roth could offer you so much more than I could.'

'Well, she has a lot more money,' said Matthew practically. 'But I wouldn't like to live anywhere without you. Even if you do give me a hard time sometimes.'

'Poor thing!' Abby pulled his hair affectionately before withdrawing her hand. 'And I suppose you think I should have told you the truth about why your father and I split up.'

'I don't know.' Matthew looked thoughtful. 'I guess it was better this way. I mean, I never doubted that I had a father, did I?'

'Oh, Matt!' Abby could feel the prick of tears behind her eyes once more.

'Hey . . .' Matthew got up from the chair, 'don't cry, Mum! Dad's going to sort things out. He said so. He's even going to look after Aunt Hannah.'

'Aunt Hannah!'

Abby caught her breath. She had been so absorbed in

her own affairs, she had almost forgotten the old lady who was responsible for bringing her and Piers back together. Hurrying up the stairs, she burst into Hannah's bedroom, sighing with relief when she saw her aunt was wide awake.

'I will have that slice of toast now, Abby,' the old lady declared staunchly, levering herself up on her pillows. 'And why are you so red-faced? What's been happening while I've been asleep?'

'Well——' Abby drew an uneven breath, 'first of all, Piers and I are not getting a divorce . . .'

It was Sean Willis's voice that eventually interrupted them. Matthew had let the doctor in, and he came to the foot of the stairs to call Abby's name. 'Do you have a minute?' he asked. 'It's about that report we were discussing. I think I've found something that might interest you.'

The report! In all the excitement, Abby had forgotten what Sean had said he would do, and calling Matthew upstairs to sit with Aunt Hannah, Abby came down to find the young doctor raking out the grey ashes in the grate.

'Aren't you cold?' he exclaimed, indicating the dead fire. 'Miss Caldwell generally has a good blaze. Is she ill?'

'Only tired,' said Abby apologetically. 'And I haven't had time to light the fire yet. It—it's been quite a morning.'

'So I believe.' Sean's expression was rueful. 'I hear this report may not be necessary.'

Abby flushed. 'What did you hear?'

'Well, you were seen getting into Roth's car earlier on this morning,' he remarked dryly. 'And Mrs Davison said you'd already been to my house—I presume to arrest my investigations.'

'Oh, no——'

'No?'

'No.' Abby shook her head. 'I—it was Matthew. He'd gone missing. Oh, it's a long story. Please—what did you find out?'

Sean drew a folded sheet from his pocket. 'This is a copy of the report Dr Morrison gave to your husband. Do you want to see it?'

'May I?'

'Of course.' Sean handed the form over. 'Though the letter attached to it is probably more comprehensible.'

Abby unfolded the sheet with trembling fingers. It was quite old and the paper had yellowed, but it was still perfectly legible. As Sean had said, apart from Piers' name, and age, and date of birth, the scrawled medical details entered on the form meant little to her, but the copy of the letter accompanying it stated his condition quite plainly.

Abby looked up then, her eyes troubled. 'But what does this mean? How does it help?'

'Wait,' said Sean flatly, and withdrew another sheaf of papers from his pocket. 'Look at this.' He handed her a copy of an identical report, again with an accompanying letter, only this time the patient's name and personal details had been obscured. 'Go ahead,' he said. 'Read it.'

Once again, it was a similar report, and this time the letter gave a favourable result. Both patients had been examined within a few days of one another, and although the unknown patient was stated in the letter to be fifteen years older than Piers, the tests had been identical, too.

Abby shook her head. 'But what does this prove? How could the two reports become mixed, if that's what you're implying?'

Sean pulled a wry face. 'I could say very easily, with Morrison's haphazard methods of filing, but in actual fact, I don't think he was to blame.'

'Then who?'

Sean grimaced. 'Let me tell you.' He paused. 'Take a look at the heading on the two reports. They were both carried out at Alnbury General.'

'Yes.'

'Morrison sent his patients there for any examinations he was not equipped to carry out.'

'I see.'

'It's a large hospital, and it just so happened at that time that there was an epidemic of food poisoning and they were understaffed.'

'So?' Abby prompted. 'They made a mistake.'

'It certainly looks like it.' Sean shrugged. 'I would never have connected the two reports had I not found them filed together. Morrison's system!' He snorted. 'Or lack of it.'

'But even so——' Abby moved her shoulders. 'Why should you be so convinced that Piers is all right? I mean——' she coloured, 'we know he is. But why should you think so?'

Sean gave her an old-fashioned look. 'Okay, I'll get to the point. After reading the two reports, I got out the other man's medical record. He's dead now, by the way, or I might not be telling you this.' He paused. 'His reasons for asking for the examination were different from Roths. He was a man in his thirties at that time. He and his wife had been married for a number of years. They wanted a family—but they didn't seem to be making any progress.'

'I understand.'

'So he asked Morrison to set up the examination. As you saw, his result was apparently positive. But when he died last year, he and his wife were still childless.'

'Oh.' Abby breathed a sigh. 'Poor man!'

'Yes, well—that's not all I found out.' Sean frowned. 'Are you ready for the rest of it?'

'Ready?' Abby felt uneasy. 'That sounds ominous.'

'The Roths already know this.'

Abby gasped. 'What?'

'It's true.' Sean shifted a little uncomfortably now. 'After I sorted the information out, I rang Alnbury General. I know several of the doctors there, and it wasn't difficult to confirm my suspicions. Particularly when they had had a similar enquiry several weeks ago—from the Roths themselves.'

Abby blinked. 'But——'

'They were asked whether there was any chance that

an error could have been made, and enquiries were instigated. It turned out that a temporary clerk had been on duty at the time the reports were prepared. It isn't beyond the realms of possibility to guess how a mistake could be made.'

Abby shook her head. So Piers had known, or at least, had his suspicions, before he went to Germany, perhaps before she even came back to Rothside. It didn't matter now. He had had another examination and the tests proved there had been a mistake. But why hadn't he told her about this, instead of allowing her to think he had done it for her?

Perhaps he hadn't done it for her at all. The idea was a painful possibility. After meeting Matthew, perhaps he had decided he wanted his son, and after considering the pros and cons, maybe he had thought this was the only sure way to get him.

'Hey . . .' Sean touched her suddenly pale cheek with a playful finger, 'I thought you'd be pleased. About your husband, anyway. It seems to prove conclusively that Matthew is his son, and that Mrs Roth's sabre-rattling was all so much hot air.'

Mrs Roth!

At once, Abby's brain began to function rationally again. Dear God, why did she always jump to hasty conclusions? She had no reason to believe that what Piers had told her was anything less than the truth. Whereas she did have the knowledge of Mrs Roth's lies about her to convince her that if anyone had contacted the hospital, it must have been her mother-in-law. She had said she *knew*. Now Abby knew how.

'I haven't upset you, have I, Abby?'

Sean's troubled voice brought her back to the present, and looping back her hair behind her ears, Abby shook her head. 'Piers and I aren't getting a divorce,' she said, touching his sleeve gratefully. 'We worked things out this morning, and I want to thank you for everything you've done.'

'Me?' Sean gave a defeated shrug. 'I've done nothing.

Except clear the way for my best girl to give me the elbow.'

'Oh, Sean!' Abby squeezed his arm. 'I'm sure you'll find someone else. Now, let me make you a cup of coffee. It's the least I can do, when we don't even have a fire for you to warm your hands.'

'There's nothing I'd like better, but I can't.' Sean moved reluctantly towards the door. 'I've got to go and see Mrs Crossley, and I'm late already. I'll be back to see Miss Caldwell later in the week, but if there's anything more you need, just let me know.'

'Thanks, Sean.'

Abby accompanied him to the gate, and he was just striding away across the green as Piers' station wagon turned into the lane leading to the cottage. Abby felt a fluttering in her heart as the Mercedes slowed to a stop, and she turned away abruptly as Piers thrust open his door.

His longer strides soon overtook hers, and putting a possessive arm about her shoulders, he said: 'What was Willis doing here?'

Abby looked up at him nervously. 'Are you jealous?'

'You know I am.' Piers' mouth compressed. 'Let's go inside. I can't think straight when we're alone, and I've got a plan I want to put to your aunt.'

Abby shrugged and led the way into the kitchen. It was chilly; she switched on the electric fire her aunt kept for emergencies before asking Piers if he would like a drink.

'Not right now,' he said crisply, glancing about him, and then, intercepting her anxious gaze, he groaned. 'Come here,' he muttered, pulling her into his arms, and the hungry press of his mouth on hers dispelled any lingering trace of uncertainty.

It was Matthew who interrupted them, coming down the stairs with his usual noisy tread, giving Abby plenty of time to put some space between her and her husband before their son erupted into the room.

'I saw the car,' he exclaimed, smiling at his father. 'Did

you go to the Manor? Did you tell Grandmama?'

'Matt!'

His mother's reproving voice brought a wave of hot colour into the boy's face, but Piers only nodded good-naturedly. 'Yes,' he said, 'I've spoken to your grand-mother. And——' he looked at Abby as he spoke, 'she agrees with me, it would be a good opportunity for her to go and stay with her sister for a while.'

While Abby was digesting this news, Matthew grinned happily. 'Do you mean Aunt Isabel?' he asked, showing off his knowledge of his new-found relatives, but Piers shook his head.

'No, I mean Aunt Elizabeth,' he replied patiently. 'You don't know her. She lives in Australia. I've persuaded your grandmother that the hot dry air will be far more favourable for her health.'

'Oh, yes.' Matthew was engagingly innocent. 'You mean her arthritis.'

'Something like that,' agreed Piers, looking into Abby's eyes. 'Now, all that's left is arranging someone to stay with your aunt.'

Abby shook her head. 'She won't like it. That was one of the reasons she wanted me to come here. She didn't want some older woman looking after her.'

'What won't I like?' To Abby's surprise, Hannah herself spoke from the doorway at the foot of the stairs. 'Well,' she added, in answer to her niece's shocked expression, 'I was tired of waiting for that toast you promised me.'

'Oh, Aunt Hannah!'

Abby felt terribly guilty, but her aunt only clicked her tongue. 'I was only joking with you, girl,' she exclaimed impatiently. 'But do put the kettle on. I won't say no to a cup of coffee.'

Abby sighed, and turned away, and as she did so, Hannah took her seat by the fireplace and looked up at Piers. 'Well?' she said. 'What won't I like? If you mean your taking Abby back where she belongs, then you couldn't be more wrong.'

Piers smiled and then, with a revealing glance at Abby,

he squatted down beside Hannah's chair. 'Thank you,' he said. 'I know I don't deserve it. But I promise that in future there'll be no misunderstandings.'

'I'm glad to hear it.'

'What we—what *I* was about to tell Abby was who I'd arranged to come and stay at the cottage and look after you.'

'Mmm.' Hannah looked wary. 'Not that ferret-faced Mrs James, I hope. I wouldn't have her over the threshold.'

Piers chuckled. 'No, not Mrs James,' he averred firmly. 'And just in passing, I should tell Abby that Mrs James is going with my mother. To Australia, I mean.' He looked up at his wife with distracting tenderness. 'We'll find someone else, and when—*if*—they come back, Mrs James can set up house with my mother.'

'What a good idea,' remarked Hannah dryly, and Abby hid her own relief behind a tremulous smile.

'No, the person I have in mind for you is Susan,' said Piers steadily. 'Susan Harris. Her family live——'

'I know where the Harrises live,' exclaimed Hannah, interrupting him. 'Good heavens, I know her mother and her grandmother. But are you sure that's what she wants to do? I thought she was working up at the Manor.'

'She is, at present,' Piers nodded. 'But she comes from a large family, as you know, and quite recently she asked Mrs James whether there was any chance of her being taken on permanently; living in.'

'I see.'

Piers regarded the old lady inquiringly. 'Well? What do you think?'

'What does Susan think?'

'Oh, she's quite agreeable.' He paused. 'To be honest, I think she's tired of handing over all her wages every week. This way she'll gain her independence.'

'Oh, but—I couldn't afford——' Hannah began quickly, only to have Piers interrupt her this time.

'Let me do this,' he said heavily. 'It's the least I can do after—well, after everything. Please. I'd like to.'

'I'm independent too, Piers.'

'I know it. But not too independent to deny your niece the happiness that is genuinely hers,' he said quietly. 'You won't refuse me, will you? Believe me, I can afford it.'

Hannah made a sound of impatience and then looked at Abby's taut face. 'I suppose I'm going to have to humour you,' she declared, with gentle irony, and Abby flew across the room to embrace her.

It was late that evening before Abby and Piers found themselves alone in the kitchen of the cottage. It had been agreed that Susan should come and stay with Miss Caldwell the following week, after Mrs Roth had departed for Australia. Until then, Abby had insisted that she and Matthew stay on at the cottage, and Piers had had to accept it.

Nevertheless, after Hannah and Matthew had gone up to bed, Piers showed no inclination to leave. 'We still have to talk,' he said, pulling Abby up out of her chair and down on to his lap. 'You still didn't tell me what Willis was doing here this morning.'

Abby sighed. 'You may not like it.'

'Why?' Piers' fingers toyed lazily with a strand of silvery blonde hair. 'I know how he feels about you. It was obvious that morning I found you two together. Why the hell do you think I was so rude to him?'

Abby gave him an impatient look. 'Is that why?'

'Don't pretend you didn't know,' replied Piers dryly. 'So come on—why was he here today?'

Abby shivered as his fingers probed behind her ear, finding the sensitive skin that curved into her nape. 'It was about you, actually,' she confessed, lifting her shoulder involuntarily. 'After what your mother said yesterday, I—I confided in him.'

'Did you?' Piers gripped her neck, turning her face up to his. 'You're right, I don't like it.'

Abby twisted away. 'I—I had to talk to somebody. You weren't here, or at least I thought you weren't, and—and your mother hadn't given me much time.'

'The hell she hadn't!' Piers swore angrily. 'Go on, tell me the rest.'

'Well, I babysat for Sean last night. He had an emergency call and it was late when he got back. He was tired, so I made him some tea.' She bent her head. 'I suppose now you're going to think there was something between us.'

Piers looked at her for a long minute, and then he pulled her closer and buried his face in the hollow of her neck. 'God, I'm sorry,' he groaned. 'I'm a selfish bastard! I'm only thinking of myself. I guess you must have been pretty desperate to confide in anyone.'

'I was.' Abby rubbed her palm along the roughening skin of his jawline. 'I didn't know what I was going to do.' She paused. 'Sean promised to try and find the report; the report they sent from the hospital. He thought Dr Morrison might have made a mistake, since he was near to retirement and so on.'

'I see.' Piers' eyes gentled. 'And what did he find out?'

Abby hesitated. 'He thinks your report and the report of another patient were confused.'

Piers inclined his head. 'And did he contact the hospital?'

'I—yes.'

Piers put a hand beneath her chin. 'Then I guess he found that my mother had been doing some investigating of her own.'

Abby gave him a worried look. 'How do you know that?'

'She told me herself, this morning. After we'd straightened things out about you and me.'

Abby was anxious. 'Was she very angry?'

Piers touched the corner of her mouth with his lips. 'No,' he said flatly. 'I was.' He shook his head. 'To think she knew the truth about Matthew's identity and didn't tell me!'

Abby expelled her breath unevenly. 'She didn't talk to you?'

'No.' Piers stroked her lips with his thumb. 'But I was

beginning to have my doubts anyway.' He gave a rueful
sigh. 'Primarily, because I wanted an excuse to take you
back.'

'Piers!'

'Well, it's the truth.' She could not doubt his sincerity.
'That morning—*the* morning I came to the cottage after
our encounter at the station—I wanted you then, and
you knew it. God, I was furious afterwards, for making
such a bloody fool of myself!'

'But when you came to London you brought Miss
Langton.'

'As protection, I think,' he confessed, rubbing his cheek
against hers. 'Didn't you think it was odd that I should
have driven Val to London, when previously she'd caught
the train?'

Abby shrugged. 'I didn't think about it.'

'Well, anyway—finding you there, realising the problems Matthew was creating, I knew I couldn't walk
away—from either of you. Taking responsibility for the
boy was a brainwave, a way to get you back to Rothside
without committing myself in any way.'

'But—you like Matt?' Abby was anxious.

'Like him?' Piers drew her lips to his and for a moment
there was silence between them. Then, setting her free, he
went on: 'I'll never forgive myself for doubting his identity. He's my son. I love him. And I'm lucky to have been
given a second chance to show him how much.'

'It may not always be easy.'

'I know that.'

'He—there may be times when he resents you.'

Piers acknowledged this. 'I know I'm going to have to
tread carefully. I know going to Abbotsford will lose its
appeal.' He took her face between his hands. 'But you
and I will be together. We can help him.' He kissed her
nose. 'You're forgetting, there may be times when I'll
resent him too.' He shook his head. 'For having you all to
himself for far too many years.'

Abby slipped her arms around his neck. 'I thought I'd
never be able to forgive you.'

'And can you?'

'Oh, yes.' Abby was very sure about that. 'It was just the same for me as for you. I didn't know how I was going to bear living in Rothside, knowing you were married to somebody else. Perhaps your mother was doing me a favour. Perhaps she realised seeing you with some other woman would tear me apart.'

'I think she realised that even if I did marry Val, I might not be the most faithful husband with you around,' retorted Piers roughly, his hand sliding possessively over her breast. Beneath the thin wool of her sweater, the nipple hardened instinctively, and this time when his mouth met hers it was with urgency and passion. 'Dear God, I want you, Abby. Let's go to bed.'

Abby gazed disbelievingly at him. 'Here?'

'You do have a bed, don't you?' he enquired, a trace of humour twisting his lips, and Abby nodded.

'But it's only a single divan——'

'Since when did we need a double bed?' responded Piers, pushing her off his knee and getting to his feet. 'You don't want me to go, do you?'

'You know I don't, but——'

'Bed,' he said huskily, pushing her towards the stairs, and with a helpless smile, Abby obeyed.

Some time later Abby opened her eyes to find Piers propped on one elbow beside her, watching her with adoring eyes. 'You're the only woman I've ever known who looks good asleep or awake,' he said softly, taking care not to disturb the rest of the household.

Abby knew a moment's regret. 'I—I suppose you've known a lot of other women,' she murmured, remembering all those lost years, and Piers bent to bestow a searching kiss on her parted lips.

'I haven't been a monk these last eleven years,' he admitted, 'but there's never been anyone else. Not in the way you mean,' he assured her.

'There was Miss Langton,' Abby reminded him tautly, but Piers only shook his head.

'Val and I never got as far as sleeping together,' he told her huskily. 'Believe it or not, we were just good friends. I think her mother had warned her she'd be foolish to get involved with me before my divorce was finalised. Anyway, it's the truth. I wouldn't lie to you.'

'But you wanted to,' Abby ventured, needing to know, and Piers gave her a wry look.

'I guess I wouldn't have objected, if she'd been willing,' he conceded honestly. 'But that was before you came back, disrupting all my carefully controlled emotions.'

Abby relaxed, putting her arms above her head and stretching like a cat. She felt as if the last weight had been lifted from her, and her arms slipped around Piers' neck as he bent to kiss the scented hollow between her breasts.

'I'm going to make arrangements for us to go away,' he murmured, drawing her close against his warm body. 'At first I thought just the two of us, but I guess it would be mean to leave Matthew behind.'

'Go away?' Abby's brows arched. 'Go away where?'

'I thought—Fiji, or the Seychelles,' Piers admitted softly. 'Somewhere hot. Where we don't need too many clothes. Somewhere we can be alone.'

'A second honeymoon, you mean?' she breathed, remembering the two ecstatic weeks they had spent in Antigua twelve years ago.

'Does it appeal to you?'

'You know it does.'

'Good. I'll fix it. Then, when we come back, we'll find a replacement for Mrs James.'

'And fix up the nursery,' sighed Abby, wriggling close against him. 'You do want another child, don't you?'

'As many as you like,' agreed Piers, his leg sliding between hers. 'But right now, all I need is you . . .'

THE WILD BEAUTY OF NORTHUMBERLAND

Piers Roth, the hero of *Season of Mists,* has an estate in Northumberland—a fitting home for this passionate and unpredictable man. For Northumberland is a place of savage beauty and breathtaking contrasts.

Situated in the far northeast of England, much of Northumberland county is rolling hills and high moorland. The enchanting Cheviot Hills run along the county's northern border and form part of the boundary between England and Scotland. These hills provide shelter for numerous little stone villages where visitors might well find themselves having a pint in a pub that has remained essentially unchanged for six hundred years! Northumberland also has an extensive and picturesque coastline marked by beautiful sandy beaches and quaint fishing villages. Visitors mustn't miss the chance to sample kippered herring, a favorite local dish.

Northumberland has a long and stormy past. The Romans of the first century A.D. were the first people to colonize the area; their legacy is the famous Hadrian's Wall, in Northumberland's northwest, built in A.D. 120–123 to keep out the savage native Picts; parts of the wall still stand today. The Danes invaded the area in the Dark Ages and their influence is still heard; Danish-speaking visitors to Northumberland today can be understood, so strongly did their ancient ancestors influence the local dialect. In the Middle Ages the area suffered extensive damage during the long and bloody border wars. Northumberland is strewed with ruined castles, fascinating relics of the devastation inflicted by warring nobles.

Northumberland's remoteness in England's far north has caused it to be frequently left off the traveler's itinerary, and this is unfortunate. For even the fussiest of vacationers will be delighted and entranced by this wild, historic and beautiful region.

Legacy of PASSION

BY CATHERINE KAY

A love story begun long ago comes full circle...

Venice, 1819: Contessa Allegra di Rienzi, *young, innocent, unhappily married.* She gave her love to Lord Byron—scandalous, irresistible English poet. Their brief, tempestuous affair left her with a shattered heart, a few poignant mementos—and a daughter he never knew about.

Boston, today: Allegra Brent, *modern, independent, restless.* She learned the secret of her great-great-great-grandmother and journeyed to Venice to find the di Rienzi heirs. There she met the handsome, cynical, blood-stirring Conte Renaldo di Rienzi, and like her ancestor before her, recklessly, hopelessly lost her heart.

LP-1

Take these 4 best-selling novels FREE

Yes! Four sophisticated, contemporary love stories by four world-famous authors of romance FREE, as your introduction to the Harlequin Presents subscription plan. Thrill to **Anne Mather**'s passionate story BORN OUT OF LOVE, set in the Caribbean.... Travel to darkest Africa in **Violet Winspear**'s TIME OF THE TEMPTRESS....Let **Charlotte Lamb** take you to the fascinating world of London's Fleet Street in MAN'S WORLD....Discover beautiful Greece in **Sally Wentworth**'s moving romance SAY HELLO TO YESTERDAY.

Harlequin Presents...

The very finest in romance fiction

Join the millions of avid Harlequin readers all over the world who delight in the magic of a really exciting novel. EIGHT great NEW titles published EACH MONTH! Each month you will get to know exciting, interesting, true-to-life people.... You'll be swept to distant lands you've dreamed of visiting..... Intrigue, adventure, romance, and the destiny of many lives will thrill you through each Harlequin Presents novel.

Get all the latest books before they're sold out!
As a Harlequin subscriber you actually receive your personal copies of the latest Presents novels immediately after they come off the press, so you're sure of getting all 8 each month.

Cancel your subscription whenever you wish!
You don't have to buy any minimum number of books. Whenever you decide to stop your subscription just let us know and we'll cancel all further shipments.